DAVID ADAMS RICHARDS

NIGHTS BELOW
STATION STREET

D0047646

An M&S Paperback from
McClelland & Stewart Inc.
The Canadian Publishers

An M&S Paperback from McClelland & Stewart Inc.

First printing September 1989

Copyright © 1988 David Adams Richards

Canadian Cataloguing in Publication Data

Richards, David Adams, 1950-
Nights below Station Street

(M&S paperback)
ISBN 0-7710-7461-1

PS8585.I17N53 1989   C813'.54   C89-094039-8
PR9199.3.R523N53   1989

Cover design by K.T. Njo
Cover illustration by Joe Fleming

Printed and bound in Canada

McClelland & Stewart Inc.
The Canadian Publishers
481 University Avenue
Toronto, Ontario M5G 2E9

"Everyone wants to change the world; but no one will change themselves."

LEO TOLSTOY

"There is blood on their lips, you fight back, and it's you they blame."

from *Vampires*, ALDEN NOWLAN

1

It was the Christmas of 1972. A spruce tree was decorated in the corner of their living room against the pine-board wall. There was a smell of evening. Their house was below Station Street and down beyond the hospital.

Adele said she never got anything. She went to bed before Midnight Mass, and then on Christmas morning got into a fight with her father and refused to open any of her presents, and instead sat on the stairs in her housecoat complaining about bad nerves and upsetting feelings.

Joe was not drinking for the first Christmas in years. But Adele said that he would probably ruin it some other way, or in some other fashion. She was waiting for him to go for the bottle any second. He was a large heavy-set man, with a clumsy stride. He went out onto the street, a street that overlooked the river, near the rocks; and while Rita watched from an upstairs window, leaning back as if frightened that he'd see her. He paced back and forth. And there was a whistle from the mill.

Rita liked to drink, but because Joe was not drinking she only had a few glasses of wine. And she was nervous too. She did not know why her husband was staying sober. But she was afraid that she was going to do something or say something to cause him to drink. She did not know what she would do or say – only she was sure she would. The last time he got drunk he had lit his pants on fire, falling asleep on the couch with a cigarette burning. Adele had woken up and, screaming, had run to the bathtub to get a plastic bucket filled with water. But she did not throw it on his pants. Instead she threw it at him, and it hit him in the face. This happened two months ago, on Hallowe'en.

Adele was already bored and depressed. She wanted to go back to school. When they brought her her presents, with her little sister Milly begging her to open them, she kicked at them with her toes, which she was busy painting.

Everyone else got a telephone in their room and she had been hinting to Rita to get her a telephone. But Rita had gypped her. Adele screeched at the television for getting blurry and then went into her room. Even the music from the radio depressed her at this moment.

Adele would ignore Joe as she went about the house, and Joe would take out a cigarette and light it as she went by, nodding to her now and then. Once when he nodded to her she flew into him again and said that yes she was quite familiar with him, she already knew who he was. Then she smirked. And then she turned on the balls of her feet and marched off triumphantly upstairs.

Ralphie came to the house and brought Adele her presents; he was tall with red hair. He had started going with her that fall, when she was fifteen, and she already had pictures of him in the house, two in her bedroom, one in the living room, and one more on the small dark paint-

8

chipped commode in the bathroom, which she wouldn't allow anyone to touch.

He stood at the door in a brand new pair of boots. His boots looked ridiculously new to her and he nodded seriously at whatever Joe or Rita said.

The first time Ralphie got to talk to Joe (this was while Joe was still drinking), Adele had spoken in a rush: "This is Joe – here – he's my father – my mother's out earning our keep selling Amway." Then she turned to him as Joe came forward to shake his hand. Ralphie had been hearing of Joe Walsh since he had been a little boy. He had heard that he hurt his back, and though he could still be called strong, and could still be capable of tremendous strength, he was acting at about half of what he had once been. Everyone in town had told him this also.

"We want to be alone, Joe – go in the other room," she said and then she began to walk about the kitchen table wiping it up.

"I'm sorry to hear your dad died," Joe said to Ralphie.

"Yes – well, go in the other room, Joe," Adele said again, blushing.

Joe smiled slightly and he went into the other room. But as soon as he did, Adele had nothing more to say, became absolutely silent, and stared at the clock. Every time Ralphie spoke she would nod and look up at the clock, as if to say: "God this visit sure is taking a long time."

Then Joe came out a few minutes later with some pictures in his hand. "Here," he said to Ralphie, "I have some pictures I'd like you to see of my camp at Brookwall."

"Well, he doesn't want to see them," Adele said, still looking up at the clock. When Joe went to hand them to Ralphie, Adele became so upset, so angry that she grabbed the pictures out of his hand and they fell and scattered over the floor.

9

"There," she said. "Well, now look at what you've done – and you've always done things just like that – "

But then she jumped off the seat and began to crawl about the floor. Joe stood in his sock feet looking down at her. And then her temper flared:

"You haven't done any exercise for your back but then Wally Johnston wants you to lift an engine and you're over at the house at midnight covered in shit and wrestling with a goddamn truck engine – *ha ha* – *ha ha* – *ha ha ha*, your old back might just fall off some day. And then Mom will have to keep shitty diapers for the rest of her life – but you won't mind that because it will give you a chance to play pinball – which is all you seem to want to play lately."

Ralphie was standing against the kitchen sink with his eyes lowered.

"Don't be rude," Joe stammered.

"Ha," Adele said flaring up. "Rude – why don't ya slap my cheeks off or stick a fork in my bum like ya did when ya were drunk. If it weren't fer Mom we'd all be on the welfare – the whole herd of us would be downtown in the office – like Jesus Frenchmen."

"I might slap ya," Joe said. He looked worried and curiously at Ralphie for a moment – as if at that moment he had no idea what Ralphie was doing in the house or why he was listening to the conversation.

"Well – and even these pictures Mom don't want you to maul and put a gross amount of fingerprints all over – and I don't care," she finished up, screaming.

Then suddenly she stood, handed the pictures to him, and smirked. She had two big barrettes in her hair, both of butterflies, which looked as if they had just lighted there and were about to carry her away.

Then she sat down again and as soon as Joe went out of

the room she hauled a cigarette out of the top pocket of her blouse and got Ralphie to light it.

She smoked her cigarette quickly with jerking movements of her thin right hand, snapping gum, and glancing towards the other room to see if he was coming back out.

"Joe's a big stupid drunk," she said. "Too bad, but that's the way it is – I never mention er as you can see – but it looks pretty grim. As far as I'm concerned, it looks pretty grim. How grim do you think it is, Ralphie?"

"I'm not real sure," Ralphie said.

"Pretty fucking grim around this place," Adele said, her mouth twisted unnaturally suddenly. "And I'm not the kind a girl to swear."

Then she smiled, butted her cigarette, and blinked quickly as if her eyelashes were stuck.

Adele now led Ralphie about the house. As they moved from the kitchen to the living room, she held onto his hand and looked angrily at everyone, especially at her little sister Milly, who had run over to him as soon as he came into the house – as she did with every new person that came in.

Later, when he got up to go, Adele led him to the door and looked at everyone, with her hair in a small net and her slippers sliding on the floor, with the same look of recrimination. Her eyes were large and blue. For some reason the whole time he was there these eyes stared about at everyone in disappointment.

Trying not to be in her way, her mother stayed in the kitchen.

But Ralphie's boots caused Adele to fly off the handle. Why hadn't her mother thought to bring them in out from the porch. She accused Rita of leaving them in the porch just because they were Ralphie's, and if they had been anybody else's it was certain they would have been brought in where it was warm. Her whole façade of acting grown up when Ralphie was there was lost, and she stormed off to her room, hitting Milly on the head as she went by.

Rita told Ralphie to come back the next day, and told Adele to stop punching Milly, and roared at Milly when she went to bite Adele on the leg.

Ralphie went, and stared back at them from the sidewalk, which was no more than a track in the half blotted-out snowbanks. Snow fell against his red hair as he stood there.

"I don't care," Adele yelled. "I can't have one friend in this here house ever in my whole life without someone trying to do something – and not one of ya take that inta consideration."

On Boxing Day, Adele walked about in her leotards, and Rita had to tell her a dozen times to get dressed because Ralphie was coming to pick her up for supper at his house, and she shouldn't be walking about half naked. Rita stood by the sink, with her arms hanging at her sides, and the washing machine going again.

When Ralphie did come she showed him her presents, and at everything she showed him, she said:

"This here isn't nothing compared to what I got last year." Or, "This is from Myhrra – she tries hard, but she never gets me anything I want. She's divorced, and just lives over there."

When Adele was showing Ralphie her gifts, Joe came into the room for a second and stood looking at them.

"And Joe got me a lot of stuff that ain't here yet," Adele said.

Joe was walking about with a cane because of his leg. Or was it his back. No one was quite sure. They were only sure that something was the matter, but as yet they had not found out exactly what. And yet today he wouldn't admit that his leg was sore. He had also picked up his first chip at AA – that is, his one-month chip – but he would not tell anyone, even Rita, that he was going. So none of his family knew why he was staying sober this Christmas, and everyone was on pins and needles, sure that at any moment a taxi would come up to the door with a load of booze.

Joe had always tried to get Adele the best present he could, and yet never seemed to have the money to do it. This year again he was planning to buy her something special, but when it came time to buy it, he only had fifteen dollars on him.

She took Ralphie about the tree and showed him the bulbs she had placed on it.

As she took him about the tree she said: "Milly put these ones here on – all in a mess – and I was coaxed to put this one on and this here one here. I like putting on the higher up ones."

"And who put on that one up there?" Ralphie asked.

"He did," Adele answered.

"Who's he?"

"Him as all."

"You mean your dad."

"Of course him. He did, yes," Adele said. Then she

13

paused and breathed through her nose, her lips went as thin as a chalk line.

"Him – he did – him!"

Sometimes when she got home late from school, walking in like a ghost – which had become something of her trademark about the house – Rita would be waiting for her, and an argument would start over something. Where did you go? Who were you with? What in god's name do you think you are doing? You have a home to come to. Do you know what time it is? I hope you're not on that jeesless dope! And Adele coming to life would answer just as swiftly and saucily as possible: Nowhere, no one, Adele, home is a pigsty. It's Atlantic time, no dope yet. And then Rita would chase her into her room with a broom.

Then from behind the door she would tell Rita that she didn't care, that it was no use, that everything was miserable in this life and that the world was going to end before too long anyway. So what did it matter?

"Well the world isn't going to end this instant – and I want you to clean up your room and pick up your good slacks and panties."

"The world might end this instant," Adele would screech, "so who cares about it."

Their neighbour Myhrra was often over to the house when these arguments erupted. With a cigarette in her mouth, and her hair tinted blonde, she would come over to talk about Mike, her ex-husband. Sometimes she and Rita would fight and she wouldn't be seen for a month or so. Then she would come back, some winter night – sending her son Byron in first, and then three or four minutes later

14

she would appear, her face red from the cold, wearing white slacks with black boots that were zippered on the side.

Myhrra often took Adele's part – to show that she understood the concerns of teenagers better than Rita.

Rita would feel outnumbered and Adele would feel an increase in her own status about the house, and she would walk about with a pompous little shrug of her shoulders telling Rita that she was only waiting for Ralphie to come and then they would take off in the Volkswagen for Calgary – the one place she wanted to go.

"How are you feeling today?" Myhrra would say to Adele, keeping Rita at a distance. Adele would crouch down in the corner and look at her fingernails gloomily as if trying to stave off temptations to bite them. Wet snow would fall against the window, and melt.

"I don't feel very well at all," she would sniff.

"Upset, are you dear?"

"I have melancholy feelings is all," she would say. "As Mom is always down cleaning carpets at people's houses – "

"I know," Myhrra would say. "But your mom *has* to earn a living." Myhrra smelled of hair rinse and peppermint, and when she smiled her false teeth would make her face slightly crooked.

Adele would rub her fingernail along her panty-hose. Her white legs scraped and her hair smelling of winter sunlight.

"Well, she has a boyfriend, and I suppose that has something to do with it," Rita would announce, looking down at them both, and trying to smile.

"Oh, Mom, are you so fooled by everything? I'm not talking about boyfriends – and I'm certainly not speaking about Ralphie, who is about as smart as Einstein, so I won't bother speaking about him in this here house ever again. I have melancholy feelings – and," she would say, screeching, "there is a load of dumps and pollution-making mills wherever you go!"

There would be a pause.

"And," Adele would say, smirking knowingly, "every time I come home something is going on and Dad is always away and you have a big brood of brats hanging onto yer legs. There is always something – and Myhrra knows what I'm talking about – so I'm getting the frig out of here as soon as possible and starting my own life where there will be no such things as loads of kids and a father who stutters his head off whenever he talks to anybody half important, embarrassing his family to death. Like meeting an M.L.A. and asking for a job."

And, saying this, Adele would look at Myhrra who would in turn keep Rita away. Sitting on the floor and surrounded by people who worried about her, it seemed to Adele that everything she said was true, and that they were making a fuss over her because she was special, and that Joe was a stuttering bully, and that she would be special as long as they made a fuss over her – or at least as long as Myhrra was there.

"And," Adele would say finally, "Myhrra, you have friends, and Mommie has none – and that's what I'm talking about time and again!"

Sometimes Joe would come home from downtown with his pockets filled with applications he had gotten from the unemployment office.

He would sit about on a snowy day filling them out while

16

Milly sat beside him or rocked back and forth on the floor. Adele would walk by now and then and say:

"Milly, roll over and play dead. Okay, now roll the other way. Okay, now sit up – okay, now speak, no don't really speak – but speak, with your paws up. Okay, now scratch fleas, now kick your hind legs up."

Then, bored with this, she would rummage through the fridge and take out a number of things, setting them on the table. Now and then she would look at her father quizzically as if wondering what it was he would be doing. Joe couldn't write very well and so often printed out his applications.

"What does the A say, Joe?" Adele would snip, chewing on an apple as the snow fell over the oil barrel outside.

"The A says Angus, Delly. My middle name."

"Ha some foolish; boilermaker mechanic – what's that?"

"That's what I am – "

"H'm?"

"Well," Joe said almost apologetically, "I was a millwright when I worked at the mines, and I worked in the woods, and I was a diver when I was in the navy – so I guess I'm not just a boilermaker – but that's the application I'm filling out."

"Pretty poor job, is it?"

"No, Delly, it ain't such a poor job – this job, if I get it, is eighteen thousand."

"Then you won't get it."

Joe, his sandy red hair receding, and his shoulders sloped down, shrugged. His black heavy pants came over unlaced work boots.

At certain times Adele would go downtown after school, carrying her books in her folded arms, her tam down over her ears, and would see him going into the unemployment office or coming out of it. The streets would be wet with

17

dirty snow, and boys would call to her as she passed. Each time she saw Joe downtown she was scared he was going to be drunk, and would pretend not to recognize him.

One day she saw him talking to Vye McLeod. Vye was standing with some groceries in his arms, and looking in the other direction as Joe explained something. There were pencils, pens, and punch-board tickets in Joe's pocket. His shirt was opened and his chest hair was exposed to the wind. Adele, who was meeting Ruby and Janet, ran into Zellers and stood behind a coat rack so Joe wouldn't see her.

The winter before, Joe managed to get some welding, and two or three times he'd come home with a flash. When he did, he would come home and lie on the couch, and Rita would put tea bags on his eyes. He had sideburns that were cut off at the centre of his cheeks, his cheekbones were large and his face was massive. At times he grew a beard.

He would lie there with tea bags on his eyes, and every now and then he would take them off, blink, and say:

"I'm still blind – who are you?"

"Terra."

"Terra – how are you, darlin?"

"Fine – why do you have tea bags up on your eyes, Joe?"

"Cause I'm blind."

He would lie on the couch with a look of complacency and two tea bags bulging out of his eye sockets, as Rita took a measuring cup filled with water and watered them down to keep them soggy.

He would just lie there with tea bags on his eyes, and try to get as comfortable as possible.

*

18

During the day the house was always open. Children from further away used it as a resting point on their way to and from school. People came in to stand and talk. Rita took care of other people's children. It was not unusual to see her carrying about more than two at a time. Children from Skytown below them, or Station Street above, would parade through her doors any time of day. It was unusual not to see three or four kids waiting around the sunlit metallic kitchen table, still in their coats and boots, waiting for Milly, or more often than not, just talking to Rita. Rita would walk about the house all day long, half undressed, picking kids up, and setting them some place else as she walked, smoking a cigarette, and talked to them without taking a breath.

"Milly, wipe your nose – wipe it; here we go – now blow, blow, not so hard, you'll walk around unbalanced and deaf for the rest of your life."

"Byron, Evan told me you scored a goal last night – well, I have it marked down." Here she would go to the kitchen drawer and take out a scribbler, in which she kept a record. "Well, that's one goal and two assists. Last year at this time . . . let me see."

"I had fourteen goals last year at this time," Byron would say, with a shift of his arms. Byron was Myhrra's son. As he talked with Rita, he would disperse the younger children with a karate chop, or grab their cheeks in his big pudgy hands and try to make their lips look like guppies.

At home, Byron had his own recreation room where he raised tropical fish in five tanks. Sometimes he would charge admission to the rest of the children to watch him feed his snakes. Sometimes in the summer Myhrra would leave him for the weekend and tell him to go to Rita and Joe's. Then she would leave twenty dollars on the counter for spending money. Their trailer was at the top of the lane, and from where he sat on the hammock he could see everything that went on. He would laze in the hammock, eating ice cream with a bored expression on his face. Children would gather around him watching the ice cream disappear. He would tell Milly to rush home and make him a ketchup sandwich. He would then ask Evan to eat the crusts of this sandwich, and if he didn't eat the crusts he would not be allowed to stay in his yard.

Evan always left the yard, and Byron seemed to get angrier than ever when he did. Bits of bread lay under the hammock as he stretched out like a beetle in a cocoon. Sometimes Milly said that she would eat the crusts if he wanted her to, since it was just a game, but Byron would look at her, shielding his eyes from the sun, and tell her he wasn't interested in what she ate.

Rita then took charge of them all. People pawned kids off on her from all over town. Five would be sitting on a couch yelling and screaming, two more would be sleeping, and Rita, throwing socks and underwear over her shoulder, picking up a load of wash and resting her chin on it as she carried it towards the basement door, would have to step over two or three sitting on their bums on the kitchen floor. She would have to keep picking them off the counter as she slogged off to do another wash, and she would be heard screaming at them and telling them to stop putting their arms in the toilet.

"No you didn't – marked in red, see." She'd hold the scribbler up.

Then at times Joe would be laid up because of his back and she would have to tend to him.

"Goddamn it all, Joe, you're not getting out of that bed!"

"I have to see about Mrs. Burke's furnace – "

"If you get up – I'll punch you in the goddamn head."

Half the time Rita wore black slacks with the zipper

broken and pinned with a big white safety pin. Her shirt was missing some buttons, and her hair was tied at the back and hung in a ponytail. Her breasts were large in proportion to her body.

She'd grown up down river. She went away for a while after graduation – to the teacher's college – but she left without her diploma. That was fifteen years ago. She had gotten married in the fall, fifteen years ago, and ever since then she did housework for other people, or took care of their children.

When she did not have children to keep, she would sometimes go out and work cleaning house for Gloria Basterache, or for two or three other women on the river.

2

Myhrra was doing all she could to get Byron to stop saying he was going to go and live with his father – and she took to bribing him. She would make milk shakes for him in the morning, and fudge to take to school. She would send away for books on tropical fish. And one night when his supper wasn't french fries, hamburgers, and Coke, he ran into his bedroom and knocked over one of his tanks. Later that night, while he slept, Myhrra in her blue jeans, and with her eyes still made up, was down on her knees picking up the fish. For the first time, Myhrra was beginning to think of getting married again.

She worked at the Central beauty salon downtown, and would keep trying to get her regular customers to come in more often. She'd take her number directory out and call them.

"Mrs. Whalen – hair must be getting long, is it?" Then she would pause, listen, rub her nose, while Byron sat over in a chair watching her listlessly, and she kept her hand up ready to shoo him away. "Listen, why don't you come in for a cut – "

Pause.

"Well . . . no I don't think it's too early . . . you've not been in in a while . . . no I didn't hear that . . . well that's just the . . . yes . . . isn't it . . . and he did, slapped her mouth off over a dill pickle . . . yes of course I knew he was as crazy as a bat in a bottle, but I never knew he'd go snakie over a dill pickle . . . come on in tomorrow and we'll talk all about it . . . I have a surprise for you . . . oh . . . new boyfriend . . . well maybe new boyfriend – Vye McLeod; we'll see if it's for real or not . . . no no, it's okay then if you can't make it."

Byron would sit there listening to her while he looked about bored and intolerant. He would haul a mouse out of his shirt pocket and kiss it, or he would suddenly squeak his shoes loudly on the floor to get her attention, and when she looked at him he would say under his breath: "Get the christ off the phone. You are making a damn fool of yerself."

Myhrra had almost gone to university. In fact she had her father haul her trunk out to the car and drive it to Fredericton. But then she decided to marry Mike, and she wanted to so badly nothing could prevent her. Her parents even tried to bribe her, but it didn't work. They said that if she just went to university for one year she could marry him and they would give her the best wedding ever. But there was something about the doorknob. As she stood in her room almost acquiescing, she heard the rattle of her father's keys to the dry cleaners, which he always carried in his pocket. It was the rattle of those keys along with the way he turned the doorknob. She had a chair propped up against it, and was standing in the centre of the room with a shoe in her hand, and her nose was running. It was the way the doorknob turned that made her marry Mike.

So once she married him nothing could have been less unusual. The little wedding took place with fifty guests. Everything was done the exact way it had to be done, and she was Mrs. Mike Preen. And her father had to go back to the university, go to the Registrar and see about getting her tuition back, and then haul her trunk down the steps of the women's residence and take it back home. And yet, just when that happened, there was such a finality about everything that she wished she had not gotten married, and she wished she had listened to her parents. She wished she hadn't seen the doorknob turn in just that way.

Mike liked to kick her in the bum and slap her around then. And she started to dye her hair and go downtown and hide on him as he went looking for her in his Monte Carlo – the very car that she had liked so much she now hid from.

Sometimes she saw her ex-husband but they always ended up fighting. Since her divorce, she had been alone now three years. At first she didn't think she would be alone at all, but her friends seemed gone now and all the years had trampled over other years, and seemed to have gone by. She had lost her teeth in an automobile accident when she was twenty-two. She had never gotten used to that, and she was afraid to smile.

She had been a beauty queen at the annual exhibition and later she had gone on a trip – and what a trip it was. They saw Seaworld and Captain Marvel. And she thought she would always go on trips and see things. But now that was fifteen years ago. A train went by in the morning and one in the evening, and she had gotten so she would run to the back door and look at it. The trailer was close enough to the tracks that it shook. And her pains bothered her –

she had a sore kidney, and sometimes when she thought she had to pee she didn't at all.

They were all young that night when she got into the car accident. Her friend Leroy flew out of the windshield and landed on the asphalt. There was a smell of burnt tin, and in the distance part of a broken windshield. When they found Myhrra, she was jammed between the front seat and the dash, still singing. Her mouth had been cut – so even now she had a little scar. They took her to the hospital and she was laughing hysterically. She was talking to Leroy – and he was sitting up, lighting nurses' cigarettes, and comforting everyone else about him. And then he grabbed Myhrra and began to dance. Later that night he went into a coma – and he died. After the accident she had trouble and peed the bed. After she was married her husband used to make her wear plastic pants, and for a while he would sleep in a chair over near the door, with the blanket up over him.

It was boredom that drove Myhrra to become a hospital volunteer this winter. She went there and visited the sick, brought them magazines and read their letters to them. The magazines themselves were two or three months old. Some of the letters had been read before. Some of the people were catheterized, and lay silently under the lights. Some would grow weaker from one visit to the next. And some would look at her suspiciously, and be angry about something.

Dr. Hennessey did not approve of the volunteer program, which was new. He was an old man who looked at her sternly and scared her every time she went there. He'd been in the war, and yet in his manner there was such an overwhelming sense of kindness that she could not be upset with him for long.

His hands shook, and his feet clomped about from one room to the next. He walked about the hospital cursing under his breath, with a nurse following him. People were generally frightened of him. He got into an argument with one old fellow who said he liked it when the volunteers dropped by to see him.

"Well, you shouldn't," Dr. Hennessey said.

"Why not?"

"Just because you shouldn't like them – you should want to be all alone rather than have them coming by."

"You don't like them, doctor?"

"Sure – sure they're the very best, boy – the very best."

And with that, he cut off his conversation and walked down the hall, breathing heavily, smoking in the non-smoking sections.

"Myhrra," he would say to her, "you should go home."

"What do you mean – I'm scheduled to sit with Mr. Salome." And she would haul out a list and show him. He would take the paper, look at it at arm's length and say:

"Well, perhaps – but he's asleep – and mostly dead – and perhaps it's best if you just go home now." Then he would smile and say: "I like your new patent leather shoes." And clumsily she would look up at him in the dark, and clumsily he would walk away.

Over everything in town rose the hospital, the station, the church, and the graveyard. Below, the river rested, beyond the woods and through the centre of town. Old buildings were being slowly replaced, being torn away, their steps faded, their pane-glass windows looking glib in the winter light.

As time went on, the doctor felt less a part of things and more by himself. Some days he would see as many as one hundred patients and find himself being rude to almost everyone. Things were changing. Now, nurses coming out of university talked about units of time, and time-units per patient. This not only bothered the old doctor, but made him sceptical of everything. He found it more and more irritating as he went on his rounds. He didn't like the nurses or the nurses' union, and had no love for unions in general. In a strange almost impractical way the nurses liked him a good deal, and not because he was overly kind in his comments. He went about declaring things. He declared that people should be shot if they pestered him about prescriptions for "little" ailments; and whenever a "disaster" happened with his sister-in-law Clare, he would say: "Did a disaster happen? Well, good."

The doctor bothered those he most loved, and argued with those he most cared about, but was obsessively polite with those he didn't like. With Clare and Adele, for instance, he always argued. No matter what Adele said, he would contradict. One night last fall she and her mother came down to the community centre to play bingo. Adele looked as tiny as ever with a big rainbow-coloured hat on her head. There was a fierce wind against the top of the trees, the pastures were trampled and the wagon roads already covered in snow. Below, the river widened into the bay; they could see the outside of barns, and in the houses they could see lights.

Since it was November, he began to talk about Armistice Day. Adele stood near them, listening.

"The world's going to blow up and there'll be another world war by next year," she said, sniffing.

"I hope so," the doctor said, looking at Adele, with snow suddenly blowing down from the trees, while Rita stood alongside them.

"Well, I support peace – and at least everyone else in the world is in for peace, except for a dozen or so who are into war," Adele said, holding onto her rainbow-coloured hat, and speaking up as if to be heard over the wind, and the outside door of the community centre banging.

The building was an old schoolhouse that they'd put on skids and had hauled down here a few summers before. Then Joe and a few of the men redid the inside and put a foundation under it. They had built an outdoor arena so the children wouldn't have to skate on the river, and they had horse-haulings behind it, where a team of horses was made to pull heavier and heavier loads. For some reason the doctor avoided horse-haulings until the last moment and then came over to stand by the fence and drink rum. Everyone considered the doctor a drunk because he drank with them – which they thought a doctor would not do unless he was a drunk.

"I'm not in for peace at all," the doctor said. "Peace won't do anything to help the world, as a matter of fact it will not do a thing – and we shouldn't be putting a lot of stock in it."

Then, with his face red and his head nodding to everyone who went past him, he got angry. Rita smiled and the doctor became troubled. First, because this was the first bingo Adele had come to in the evening and she was all dressed up, and her knees were shaking from the cold night wind while the bulb over the door cast light on the frozen grass. Second, because she had won a prize and held it in her tiny hands. Third, because Rita had told her not to be rude, when the doctor felt he was as obstinate as she was.

In the mornings people would come to his house to be treated. And Clare would take their Medicare numbers and make appointments. They would sit along two benches in his office, and he would come in through the other door, peer at them, and wave his hand to someone to follow him in.

"Don't be shy with me," he would be heard telling an Indian woman from down river. "I mean I'm just feeling for the baby's head. It's dropped down but it's not in position yet – so don't go driving about bumpy roads so you'll go into labour – no it's not for a while yet . . . ."

Then he would wash his large red hands, and come out again, his eyes piercing through his thick glasses:

"Make her another appointment for next Thursday," he would say.

Every now and then Gloria Basterache would come in about some complaint. Everyone could tell that she made the cross old man nervous; because whenever he gave her a check-up he would call Clare in with him.

After supper he would go to the hospital.

Some nights he would go in and out of the hospital three or four times. No one ever knew what floor he was on, where he was going to. If Dr. Armand Savard was in the hospital, Doctor Hennessey would go in and out glumly. If Dr. Savard or Dr. McCeachern got together – both youthful, both in high spirits – the doctor would become more and more glum.

Savard and McCeachern thought the old man was like

this for a variety of reasons. They supposed he was like this most of all because no one paid any attention to him anymore – not like they paid attention to themselves. The treatments he prescribed a lot of times were no longer valid. And their lives were so much better organized than his. Besides, Armand felt the old man was prejudiced against the French, and often waited for him to show his hand in that regard. Savard would look over at McCeachern, or someone else, and say: "The war – the war." And amid muffled laughter, he would tap his forehead.

When he went home to his sister-in-law Clare, whom he could never tell he loved so she'd ended up marrying his brother, he complained to her that everything was different and he may as well retire. And then in the same breath, as if holding it against himself, he would berate all people who retired, and he would say also that retirement was only the mandate of the young, which she, sitting in her plaid skirt and bobby socks, did not understand. Since his brother had died, they lived together in the same gigantic old house, built like many of the other old farmhouses, below Madgill's garage. It sat back off the road, on the left of the power-line, with green shutters, and an old porch that had three or four faded wicker chairs. There was a barn. There was some wood. There was a nailed-down coal chute, with metal stripes crossing it. The doctor's office was on the right-hand side facing the road. He had treated the whole roadway for thirty years.

Nothing was the same now, he would tell her, and yet he would say everything was the same and not one thing was different. Was it not the same thing with his nephew Ralphie as with him, and was it not the same with Vera, his niece, as it was with everyone else. Ha. Then almost spitefully he would shake his head so you could see the space between his grey hair and the collar of his shirt, and the light casting off from the snowbanks relegated to the evening air. He would take some chewing tobacco and clamp it down between his back teeth, and then he would spit.

"How do you mean?" Clare would ask.

"I mean, everything is the same and always has been and always will be," he would say, walking away.

3

Adele had begun to dye her hair and wear the tight jeans and shirts she had seen her friends wear. Yet she was never happy with how she tried to look. She felt she didn't look as good as other kids, and she was continually trying different fashions and then abandoning them. She would walk about in tight jeans showing her skinny bum, and then just as suddenly she would go a week or two without wearing jeans at all, but only dresses or skirts.

One of the memories she had of her family was that her mother picked blueberries, standing in her skirt against the background of trees that had been seared by a forest fire, and one of the men said her father couldn't lift a boulder out of the ground. Joe stood in his blue suit, coming from church, his shoes hidden, his shoulders catching the shadows of the tree's waving motion on his back and hair. Joe lifted the boulder, put it on his shoulder, and then with the other hand picked up her mother, and Rita started crying.

She often criticized her mother for being foolish enough to live with him. It seemed to her that if her mother wanted to be a fool now, and wanted to keep kids for other people – this to Adele was an insult – and wanted to make her life like she did, then that was fine, but she herself would not have any part in it, and when she grew up she would be quite different from her mother, and by being quite different, she assumed she would be better.

Therefore at home everything depressed her. The idea of Rita and the children depressed her. That Milly was off the wall, and needed to be tied to the mattress so she wouldn't run outside at night, depressed her. That her father had three tattoos on him, depressed her. That told you everything.

They once took her father to jail. It was in the evening and she went up to the window and looked in at him. And when he looked at her she yelled: "So – will they hang you or what?" Then she got giddy, stepped on a nail which punctured her sneaker, and fell flat on her face.

Adele's nerves were bad. She would not sit at the table if Milly ate beside her. She could not eat her food unless she had Kleenex piled all about her plate, to keep off Milly's breath.

When she got a bottle of pop, she would take a sip or two of it and put it in the fridge, with a note on it that read: "MILLY – I SPIT IN THIS!"

Sometimes she would complain about having nothing to wear, and Joe would say: "When's yer birthday, Delly?"

"Pardon me?"

"When's your birthday?"

"You know's well as I do – April Fool's is my numbskull birthday as I'm always getting teased bout it one way or the other from all sides of the world."

"Well, that's not too far off, is it?"

"Pardon me once more?"

"That's not too too far away?"

"Million zillion years, there about."

"Well we'll see what happens April Fool's."

"Salt gets changed for sugar and something foolishly stupid is written about in the paper about something foolish and stupid," Adele said, taking a Scotch cookie and popping it into her mouth.

Then she would walk about the house shrugging at what her mother said, or floating in and out of rooms like a ghost with her history or math books in her hands, or sitting on the window-sill waiting for Ralphie to telephone her.

In early March, Joe had gone into the hospital for a week and had come out, and was recuperating from the tests he'd had. These tests seemed to always come to nothing; and there was never anything they could really put their finger on.

Adele would end up arguing with him, and it could start over anything.

"How are you today?"

"Not so bad."

"Well why do you not go outside or something?"

"I doubt if I could walk real well right at this moment, Delly."

"Well, let me rub your back for you."

"No – go on – it's alright."

"Don't be so goddamn stubborn, Joe – let me rub your goddamn back like I used to!"

Then she would sit across from him and brood in a sort of silent, judgmental fashion. The house was filled with the scent of cigarettes. And she would tell him, with her cold face in the damp spring light, that she knew he didn't like Ralphie – she could tell, and that was the one thing about him that she could tell.

"I like Ralphie a lot," Joe would answer.

"Ralphie and I aren't getting married – we are just going

34

to live together in common law way out in the woods or something like that there."

He wouldn't answer.

"Well, what do you think of that?"

"Doesn't bother me."

"Sure it does!"

Joe would look over at her quietly.

"My parents were never married."

"That's because, Joe, as everyone in the whole world knows, you had no real parents at all," she would snip.

Rita would then come in and say something to her and Adele would smirk, yawn, and look out the window. Often, she would go to the fridge and get her pop, with the note on it saying: "I SPIT IN THIS." One afternoon Milly sat in the kitchen while Adele took her pop out of the fridge piously, and went to take a drink. Just as she got the pop to her mouth, Milly sniffed and said: "So did I."

Adele had other problems. One of them was that she had nightmares and couldn't sleep very well at all. Then she had a nervous stomach. Then a teacher looked at her in a funny way. Then something happened to her fries at Zellers – she went to sit in a booth with her allowance and they gave her cold gravy and she wouldn't eat them, and they wouldn't give her her money back. Then, because of this, she said she wasn't going to go back to school.

"I'm no one's fool," she screeched. "And I'm not going to do the dishes tonight!"

And saying this, and brightening up as if she had quite mysteriously solved everything, she ran upstairs and slammed the door.

"What have we done to you?" Rita yelled.

"Well, Rita, if you want to know the big facts of life – let me teachcha in yer dumb brain – you got married to Joe, who was a alcoholical bastard, so there!"

"So there," Rita said. "If I go up with a spatula, little lady – you aren't that big – and if I go up those stairs – "

"Come way up," Adele squeaked. "I'm not afraid of you or anyone like you – not one little Jesus bit."

"I will if you don't grow up."

"Ha, ha ha, ha haha, ha ha ha ha ha!" Adele roared.

Pause.

Rita started to climb the stairs.

"And I have nothing in this house, and am sick to my stomach all the time – don't you know that Mom – you know that Mom – I'm sick to my stomach all the time and have nervous feelings."

Rita stood halfway up the stairs looking over the top of the banister.

Pause.

Rita started to go back down the stairs.

"Like the time, ha, Dad leaves me in the woods so I mayswell have been fried by an Indian or something like that there, it'd not be impossible, or the trip we went on that Christmas – remember that, Dad, I spose you don't remember that. Or the time you took us to the circus to see the tallest man in the German army, who isn't as tall as he's made out to be – and got into a fight with Cecil, and Mom and us had to go home alone because you were locked up, and then the next day you and Cecil went out for a drink together, and if you don't remember, Dad, many thanks."

Through these arguments, Joe sat in his chair with his makins in his pocket, and his shirt half opened, listening as the day got dark, his eyes focused on the tile at the end of the rug.

One night, Milly broke out crying when Adele came downstairs with her overnight bag packed, with her scuffed buckled shoes sticking out of the top of the bag, saying she was going to run away with Ralphie Pillar. It was at this time for some reason that Adele wanted everyone to know how much she knew about sex – and now because she was angry, she told them all she knew, and all that she understood:

"I know all about it," she said, "I KNOW THE FACTS!"

Adele stood at the door, while Milly tried to grab onto her, to force her back into the house. The windows were frosted over and there was a smell of ice in the porch. Joe had gone out to get them a treat, but he hadn't come back yet. His hockey skates were tied to a nail. Milly's eyes were closed and red, and her nose was running, and her hands kept grabbing at Adele's black plastic belt, while Adele tried to pry her fingers loose. Milly was roaring at her mother to come and help, but Rita sat at the metallic kitchen table under the light bulb.

Adele turned her somewhat cold little face toward Milly and said: "When I was yer age Milly, I was in a hospital bed, and Joe was out drunk, roaring about in a goddamn fish-tailin car and slappin our mother's cheeks off every second night. So why do you think, Milly, that this place is so wonderful – h'm?"

And, with that, she walked out and slammed the door, and headed toward the centre of town, perfume on her jeans.

4

The winter and then the summer months passed, and fall
came.

Myhrra called Joe at six o'clock one morning, when it
was still dark, and told him that she knew he was asleep but
that something was broken in her car. The air smelled cool
again. The street outside was broken up. The sky was still
filled with pulp and smoke and down below on the river a
buoy light winked, saying I am not just any light but a light
from a pont-shaped river buoy.

Joe, pulling on his pants and shirt, and fastening his
large belt, coughed and lit a cigarette. Through his upstairs
window he could smell frost, and he could see the kitchen
light on in Myhrra's trailer above the dark gravel lot which
he could not see in the summer but now the leaves were
going again. Rita slept. He stepped over her clothes and
closed the bedroom door.

When Joe arrived at the trailer, Myhrra was outside and
snow fell against the pulp-field in back of them. She wore
her heavy coat over her housecoat. She sneezed and
rubbed her eyes.

"Joe," she asked him, "you've been in jail, haven't you?"

"A few times," Joe said.

"What's this jail business like?"

"Well, I was in jail for a while for breaking a window," Joe said. "After the cops came to the house – I hit one."

"Oh," Myhrra said. "What happened there, Joe?"

"Nothing," Joe said. "Rita was going to leave me. I was in a big scrape at the house. The cops took me to jail for my own good, I guess. I didn't mind er except when Delly came to see me."

Joe remembered that whole incident. It was the time he threw a chair, and it stuck into the wall at the back of the kitchen. The cops came, and after he hit one, they put the cuffs on him, and he snapped them off. The young female cop, Judy Dennifer, took her cuffs and put them on him, and he snapped them off also. The whole time he kept thinking: *If Rita wants me to go with them, I'll go.*

It was in summer. There were bags of garbage in the porch, and a lot of the house was being redone. There was paint on his hands and in his hair. He had tried not to get drunk the night before but hadn't managed to stay sober.

Then all the cops gathered about him and took him out. Everyone was on the street. Rita was crying. He saw a vindictive look on Judy Dennifer's face. He smiled at her, and then looked at the ground.

"Oh," Myhrra was saying, "pretty bad way to go, Joe, with Rita and the kids there. . . ."

Joe nodded. He smiled, and blinked. And suddenly his big face looked confused.

Myhrra sniffed and looked about and there was wind against her eyes.

"Are we all crazy?"

"Who?"

"The whole kit-and-caboodle of us."

"I don't know," Joe said quietly, and lifted up the hood.

39

Far away a mill whistle blew in the air, and far away a dog barked – and there was the faint rattle of a truck as it passed by.

Joe looked at her and smiled. He could see her bra under her open coat, and when she smiled he could see the scar above her top lip.

"Cub Master said that Byron robbed the money from the troops."

"The troops," Joe said.

"The cub troops' money. They were raising money, had a hundred dollars, but now – " here she stammered – "money is missing, and Byron was blamed."

"Well, that's too bad," Joe said.

"Sure, because he needs someone to blame it on – and it mayswell be Byron, because I'm a woman alone!" Myhrra said. She looked in at the engine as she spoke.

"Ya, that's always the way," Joe said.

"Are you drinking yet, Joe?" Myhrra said intently, inspecting the carburetor.

"No," Joe said.

"Oh no you're not – of course you aren't – I wish I could quit."

"Oh," Joe said, surprised. He knew Myhrra didn't drink.

"Yes," Myhrra said. "I'm a drunk," she said, yawning. Myhrra seemed to be everything anyone else was. A snowflake came down in the cold air and landed somewhere. One of her thumbs was blistered and had a Band-Aid around it. The dog barked again.

"Byron is smart," Myhrra said. "As ambidextrous as hell, too. Is Milly passing? Or is she flunking out like she did in kindergarten?"

Joe slapped her hand so she would take it out of the way.

"She's doing fine," Joe said. Actually he didn't know.

After this he became embarrassed, and there was a long silence while he tried to think of something to say.

"You should take care of Rita, Joe," Myhrra said, as if she had worked herself up into being sad suddenly, just as she worked herself up to be concerned when she carried those month-old magazines down the corridors of the hospital.

Joe nodded. His old canvas coat seemed to crinkle as he worked. The ice in the ditch had the same look as curdled milk, with some weeds sticking up out of it.

"Yes. She's had a hell of a time. When she was young she did floors for people," Myhrra said. "I mean, she still does, too. But this was down river. I used to have to stop people from stepping over her while she worked. I can vouch for that."

Then Myhrra told the story about how she protected Rita, and how Rita always looked up to her. It was always the same story, and she always seemed to tell no one else but Joe this story.

"Anyways," Myhrra said, "it would have been just terrible if she left you, Joe – when you were at your worst. Like a maniac."

Joe said nothing to this but nodded again.

He cleaned the battery posts off and reattached the cables and tightened them.

"Were you in the navy or army, Joe?"

"Navy."

"Was it exciting?"

"No."

"And that's where you got the tattoos?" Myhrra said.

"That's it," Joe said.

"Well, I usually hate men with tattoos, Joe – but I make an exception for you."

Myhrra then seemed to not know what else to say. Day-

41

light was coming just as it had come years ago. It smelled of ice in your lungs. Daylight flashed against the naked alders, warmed the side of the bank, and cast light on the dark below them, and Myhrra stood in an old pair of sneakers that were stiff and upturned at the toes.

"I hate hippies, Joe – don't you?" she said.

"Pardon me?"

"Hate – hippies?" She leaned against the side of the car as he worked, and looked sideways at him, her hair falling over her face.

"I don't know any hippies."

"Well, that Ralphie character – and his sister Vera – who's a real Beatnik, I heard." She paused. "Thelma Pillar's children."

"Oh," Joe said, "I never considered Ralphie a hippie."

"Well, perhaps he isn't," Myhrra said. "I just know a lot of girls that Mike's been hanging about town with that look like hippies. Split ends forever." Then she smiled sadly again, as if to herself, and stepped away quickly when Joe closed the hood of the car.

5

Ralphie, like his sister Vera a few years before, belonged to the town without being a part of it, knew all about it without people knowing him, and went about as an outsider through no one else's fault.

He was tall and thin with red hair and delicate features. Though he was tall he weighed only a hundred and twenty-seven pounds. He had gone to university for a while, and then to technical school. But then his father had taken sick. When he was visiting him in the hospital the pressure was on to do something. His father would ask him to make a stab at something, for his mother's sake. And his mother would tell him he must do something for his father who was sick. His mother was elitist and domineering. For a long while she had never been seen anywhere except at church. Neighbours would not see her all winter long because she always kept to herself. Her house would look cold and solitary amongst the other houses.

The problem was that Ralphie did not know what to do. His marks in chemistry and calculus were the highest in the province in high school, and at university he always made out with the least effort.

When his father was sick he would visit him at the hospital. It was at this point that his mother and he felt as if they weren't doing the right things, because they didn't know what to do. He would shovel the walk for his mother to get out to the hospital at night.

Every evening when Ralphie got to the hospital, Myhrra would be in the room before him. She had become a sort of friend to his father during the last few weeks of his life, and wouldn't leave him for a moment. His father could only speak in a whisper. He was dying of bone cancer. And sometimes when the nurses moved the sheets from under him, or lifted him, they would crack a bone in his shoulder, or in his arm. It had been a progressive deterioration of his bone structure for six years. And everything seemed to have been spearheaded toward nothing else but this moment.

They would go into the room, and Myhrra, sitting there, would instruct them on what had been happening.

"His fingers are all yellow tonight. And his toes – his big toe broke again – and he was calling for someone named Danny?"

"That's his brother," Ralphie said.

"Oh, what does he do now?"

"He's an optometrist," Ralphie said.

"An optometrist," Myhrra said. "Well, isn't that something." Then she would look at Ralphie as if he was bragging.

She would stare at his mother, and then begin to read, her lips moving softly.

"Who is that person?" Thelma asked once.

"She's just trying to be kind," Ralphie said. Whether he was in a hospital or not, Ralphie was always the same. His teeth were large, but seemed appropriate to his face. He seemed to be always smiling.

44

Sometimes Thelma would not go to the hospital if she thought Myhrra was going to be there. But she refused to tell Myhrra to leave, and Myhrra was determined to stay. So all through Mr. Pillar's last days, Myhrra – who had not known the family very well over the years – knew all the gruesome and hideous details of his illness, along with her son Byron.

But then, at the very last, just when Ralphie's father was expecting her to come, she had an argument with Thelma over some telephone call concerning treatment in Montreal. Myhrra had talked Mr. Pillar into asking to go to Montreal where she said they would be able to save him. Mr. Pillar got this in his mind, that he could be saved only in Montreal. Finally Thelma, along with the doctors, had to tell him that there was no possible treatment in Montreal. Because of this, Myhrra took no further interest in either of them, and went to another ward. Mr. Pillar would call her name, and look peevishly angry with Thelma, and refuse to take her hand because she had sent Myhrra away and had not sent him to Montreal. He would lie in bed, tears running down his face as they sat beside him.

After his father's death, Ralphie missed him and seemed to cling to his father's possessions – his coat that he wore, a leather flask for drinking, with a picture of the Bluenose on it. And a certain scent of the streets, at a certain time of day, and sometimes the courthouse with its iron railing and worn steps, covered in new snow with pink dying light through the windows, made him sad.

Snow came down on the streets, the buildings, the pits and props in the fields. And he and Ivan Basterache travelled about together, he drinking out of the flask and imitating others as much as possible, sometimes wearing his father's heavy winter coat, and a small blue toque. Ralphie suddenly had this affinity for Ireland, and everything

45

about him had to be Irish. He sang Irish rebel songs and drank stout, and proclaimed loudly that he was holding the memory of his father sacred by being Irish. This idea that he was Irish, and that they came over to Canada from Ireland became paramount with him, wearing the old winter coat, and having the mischievous grin.

Although Ralphie already believed that everything in the world, everyone and everything, happened exactly the way that it was supposed to, and that once something did happen, no matter how preposterous it was at first, it was meant to happen and was therefore absolutely natural, he still felt that Adele and he only became boyfriend and girlfriend because no one else seemed to think very much of them. Neither of them knew very much about how to act with these other more special and gifted people – gifted in the way people who assume they are doing all the right things – that is, socially gifted. So he and Adele ended up together. He learned that her father was a drunk and her mother was the woman who had taken care of him when he was a little boy.

Adele's body was so tiny and so skinny that perhaps he and she were more of a match than most people. Another thing that he discovered at this time – both of them were frightened of music. That is, they would go out of their way to miss a dance, or to stay away from a concert. Adele, because she thought there would be liquor there, and she hated it, and Ralphie, because he had secret fears about bullies on the dance floor since he had been beaten up.

Adele and he would stay home from the dances, or go to the movies together.

At times he would convince Adele to sneak in a bottle for him in her purse, which made them both pretend they were proud and dangerous. And it probably made Adele feel she was fitting in even though she did not drink herself. Adele would often boo the main feature so loudly that he would have to put his hand over her mouth. Adele also ate her mitts. She would sit in a movie chewing holes in the thumbs and he couldn't get her to stop doing it, so one day before they went to a movie, he put pepper on the thumbs of her two mitts, and after he did this she said she would never be able to *really* trust him.

Sometimes Ralphie earned some money by running the projectors for the night. He made changeovers and spliced reels much better than the regular projectionist, who always found something wrong with the machines after Ralphie left. This happened about twice a month, Ralphie smelling of solder, wearing rubber boots and khaki jeans, with four extra puncture holes in his belt and his hands covered with grease, and Adele sitting on a stool, kicking her feet against the tins of film.

Some time after his father's death, Ralphie took an apartment, even though his mother didn't want him to and demanded he stay with her. After two or three months, other people his age heard that someone had rented an apartment, and most of them came in and out of the apartment any time they wanted. Ralphie never stopped them from using it, and he never knew who he was going to find there. He had no idea that some would rob him, or that they would use it when he wasn't there. That they did both of these things went right past him.

But the real problem was that they soon became immune to him and treated him like it was a communal apartment, with everyone having the "same ideas" and everyone friends.

It was in the apartment that Adele met a variety of people. She went there every day after school.

People came in and out of town from university – back and forth, to and fro. Ralphie knew most of them, and had taken courses with some of them. And Ralphie's apartment became a meeting place for all of them.

Adele, not even knowing that she was doing it at times, tried to ingratiate herself with these people. She believed that what they said must necessarily be true and she began to try to dress like them, with what Dr. Hennessey called "the back-to-the-land-poor look of those who could afford it."

However, because Adele had been poor all of her life she had seen more of life by the age of sixteen than a lot of these people – or at least a lot of life some people coming from university had taken courses on and pretended to be dismayed about. It was becoming a cultural thing to be dismayed at the right times about the right things. Adele had seen and heard more of all of the things that were becoming sanctioned as the concerns of the day, but she always measured herself against these people, and always found herself lacking.

That is, the affectation of concern was always seductive, but wit and affectation most often eclipsed Adele, with her nervous stomach, her skirt with the hanging hem, and her chewed mitts.

6

For a while Ralphie listened to the voice of the men at the
N.D.P. meetings, which took place up a street on the far
side. He could see a light in the window, and he saw Burl
Thibaudeau and Dr. Armand Savard, the doctor with the
professorial look, coming and going. Sometimes at night
they would by-pass his door. Savard, with his goatee, and
Thibaudeau, with his hair hanging in front of his face.
There was the idea that there was something fresh and
new about this party, and that this party was more substan-
tial than the others.

Once in a while Ralphie would go and talk to Burl, his
old next-door neighbour. He would sit with him in the
basement of his house, and Burl would manage to bring
the conversation around to the N.D.P. and why Ralphie
should join. There was the feeling that Ralphie had now
gone on, and that Burl had remained where he was – in
the small creamery near the tracks, with its gravel and
cinder track, and its dark windows. And yet each time Burl
spoke, he spoke to Ralphie about how new, fresh, and
resourceful the N.D.P. was, with his hair hanging about his
eyes, and his wife would listen to him patiently and look

over at Ralphie every now and again as if trying to take a cue from him about her husband.

Then he would go home. Ivan Basterache by this time had moved in with him, with his knives and home-made tattoos, and his idea that Ralphie was like his father, or older brother. Ivan was sixteen and had been out on his own for quite a while. When people came in, he would run about attending them – getting them drinks, and making tea. His clothes smelled wet, and his hair was long. He looked like an innocent girl except for his bright eyes. He had "F.U.C.K." tattooed over his knuckles, and "Dangerous" scratched across his wrist. His mother was Gloria Basterache – who was a friend of Myhrra's – and he adored his mother.

All during that fall people came and went. They shot off a gun and put a hole in the wall, and one boy fell off the window ledge and landed on the porch below. A girl from up river locked herself in the bathroom one night, and poured a bath until water spilled over the floor, and then tried to do herself in by taking all her birth control pills. When they finally got the door opened, she was sitting on the tub rim, with water pouring over the enamel, with her pants and brassiere on, the top of her breasts heaving with unremittant sobs.

What they hated he pretended to hate, and what they liked he pretended to like – so in this way he and Adele fit in, and they both adopted the idea for a while that they also were not inhibited, and that they also were not jealous, and that they too were free of all of that. Suddenly, the more offhanded one was about everything, the more well informed and the better that person was. So Ralphie and Adele would pretend to each other that they were acting exactly the way they should be acting, and this way was the overall best way to act. Adele would sit on the beanbag chair and with her brown hair hanging down over her eyes take on the look of a person who had suddenly in a matter of hours grown up completely – and had been very much abused.

Adele had friends now who wouldn't speak to her two months before, and though two months ago they would have ridiculed her at school for being a "sook" – now these girls called out to her, asked her if she was going to the apartment and if there was going to be a party there. And Adele, with her skinny legs and hip bones sticking out, led these girls about as if they were her own popular crew, and throughout the fall she could not help thinking she had made enormous amounts of new friends.

Ruby was one of her friends that year and she would come to the apartment every night. Her hair was long and brown and she wore large earrings. Her face was babyish and pretty and she had a command over Adele because she was pretty. Also she was well-liked and pretended to be wild, although she got others to be wild for her. Little Cindi, the epileptic, whose father always tried to get into her pants, would wake up in the morning with one desire and that was to be as wild as the river just for Ruby, and Adele did also, because she wanted to fit in.

The favour Ruby often asked of Ralphie was could she bring a boy over in the evening. And Ralphie always said yes she could, that bringing boys over was the "very best" of an idea, except that Ruby often brought someone over who was going out with Cindi at the time. Cindi had his

51

ring, or his high-school jacket, or something else, and Ruby had him. Cindi would blink her albino eyelashes and look about hopefully, sitting in her new corduroy bibs.

Adele was abrupt with Ralphie sometimes, and had a fiery temper, but he saw that people could take advantage of her in a lot of ways, and she would play the fool for them just so she would not be left out or be regarded as different. People teased her about not drinking, and he knew it hurt her to listen to them telling her how natural it was to drink. For the longest time, she never told people about her father, or what it was that kept her from taking a drink, and she often would ask Ralphie to buy beer for Janet and Ruby. She did not want to be thought of as the person who would ruin everything for others just because she did not do it herself.

"Cheers," she would screech as they drank. "C'mon – let's clink glasses." Her eyes would blink, and there'd be grass stains on her woollen knee socks, leaves in her brown lovely hair.

Ruby and Janet took advantage of her over this very thing, and played upon it, and mixed her up, and gave her nervous feelings, and made her throw up because she thought she wasn't doing enough to please them. Adele would run about trying to please them and Cindi would follow her with peace signs all over her coat, in the damp fall air.

For some reason Cindi's epileptic seizures always got worse in the damp, and once she fell near a car outside the Basket Centre and began to twitch convulsively. Adele immediately went over to her and dragged her out of the puddle, and tried to shove a pencil in her mouth, while Ruby and Janet went into Jean's Restaurant and hid behind the coat rack. Adele kept kissing Cindi's albino eyelashes and petting her, and Cindi later on told Ruby she was sorry.

Everything at this time was exciting. There was the girl who had taken an overdose of birth control pills, and another who threatened to slash her wrists unless her boyfriend came home that night from St. Thomas University to see her, and they had to sit up with her until four o'clock while a storm blew outside. All of this made Adele feel that she had secrets to keep from her parents, that these secrets identified her as being a part of a group, that this group was more irreverent than any other group you could ever imagine – that this whole idea of irreverence was somewhat new and shocking – that she, in fact, belonged to the eight or nine people who knew that these were the right secrets to have.

Sometimes when it was high time for them to go home, and Ralphie, half dressed, was walking about trying to be polite and get ready for a carpentry class he was taking, while the dim lights from the street shone on the great bare-looking furniture and showed the long stovepipe in the early winter dark, and there was that vague smell of cinder on the ice, people would sometimes ask Adele to intercede for them. The girls would bring her into the kitchen and beg her, and hold her hands, and whisper in her ear. And like anyone else who is not used to having influence, Adele would run about trying to make them all happy. "Can Janet stay while you are out – her mother's mad at her for smokin hash."

There was the idea that they were suddenly all in hiding from their parents and desperate because of it. And Adele, without knowing it, found herself acting like a maid. Running out to the store for them in the afternoon, standing in line with them at Zellers even though she didn't need anything – and finding out that whenever they went anywhere they never actually called her. But when Ralphie mentioned this, she would get angry and it was all shoved into the corner. The trouble was Adele felt that these new friendships would last and that she was indispensable now to Ruby and Janet. She realized how they ridiculed people and exactly how they talked about people they didn't like, but as long as she was with them, and indispensable to them, they would not talk about her that way.

Upstairs, a woman named Belinda lived with her daughter Maggie. She was Vye's ex-girlfriend, and had to get up every morning at five to go across the river to work. And Ralphie, though he tried to keep everyone quiet at night, could never seem to manage it. Every time the woman saw him, she fixed him with a cold stare, and then ran upstairs, two steps at a time. And at night she would take a broom and pound it on the floor. She could not afford to move out, and the landlord never acted on her complaints or on the complaints of anyone else either.

In the afternoons, Belinda would trudge up the stairs with her groceries. With the entrance door propped open with a stick she would haul the flour up the steps as snow swirled over the welcome mat. Then she would go back down and haul the potatoes up past Ralphie's doorway where the girls would be standing waiting for Ralphie to get home and let them in. Belinda would get the box of canned goods, and then begin to carry the bags. All the while, the girls would stand at the door with morose faces. Once, as Belinda passed them, one of the girls ran down to the entranceway and kicked the stick out of the door and rushed back up the stairs. Once, when the woman had to leave a bag of flour on the second-floor landing while she went up to the third floor to open her door, Cindi, Ruby, and Janet kicked the flour back down the steps.

"Who did that?" the woman said.

"We don't know – it fell by itself."

"It did not."

"Did so."

"Did not."

"So – it fell by itself – it flopped over by itself, if ya wanta know."

"I can't afford to waste flour," the woman said.

"Then don't waste it," Janet said. "No – don't go bout wasting it."

When Belinda went up to her apartment and when she came back down she told them she had telephoned the police. She wore an old dress too tight for her legs, a big sweater, a lime-green woollen winter coat. Vye had promised to marry her at one time, and she had been hoping he would.

Because she always said she telephoned the police, and the police never came, the girls laughed. Just at that moment Adele came up the stairs: "There's Del, there's Del," they all said, with more excitement than usual, as if she would immediately know what was going on, and immediately recognize the hilarity of the situation.

Adele had no idea what was going on, but at the moment believed she did, and that it was hilarious. She burst out laughing and put her hands over her mouth. The smell of late afternoon pervaded the walls, and in the half-dark apartment building they had the feeling that this was the best place to be.

Even though Adele finally had friends now, she still became constipated and couldn't sleep, and then she became afraid that Ralphie liked Cindi, or Ruby, or even Janet, more than he liked her. She became scared that this is what the girls wanted. She remembered how Ruby once put her arm about him and laughed and winked.

Every time Adele lay down to go to sleep, she saw that wink.

In many of the things his friends said, Ralphie felt at a loss to argue with them, not because he agreed with them, but because he was only sure that he wasn't sure one way or the other. And sometimes he took a stand on things that were particularly contradictory to others in the apartment.

One of the great debates was that this generation had somehow not only invented drugs, but that everyone who did drugs was more aware of life. Ralphie – with his bottle of Paarl brandy and his father's old coat, coming back from a meeting with his mother where she cried and was angry with her dead husband because the fence boards were loose at the back of the house – would say that he didn't know if that was true.

This was the idea of certain people who came to his apartment, which gave rise to the idea, with the town police, that his apartment was a commune, and the place was raided twice in a month.

That the police could and did pick Ralphie up allowed his mother's neighbours to sympathize with her, and to feel a little gleeful that such a smart aleck – which is what they considered Ralphie to be once this happened – was getting his comeuppance.

Once, the band that played at the rink dropped in after their performance and brought in some booze, and word got around that there was a party at Ralphie's. He himself didn't hear about it until he was walking home from his mother's.

Ralphie soon found, at a hundred and twenty-seven

pounds, and wearing a great big cowboy belt, that he was not able to take care of the apartment the way he should, and whenever he visited his mother, she would always ask him to come home before he got into trouble.

*

The drapes and the furniture in Thelma's house were white. The coffee table was made of heavy glass, with round glass coasters on it. There was a smell of faint cigarette smoke in the air, but it never seemed to be in the room you were in.

Thelma would talk to Ralphie, about having to do something with his life, and having to think of his father, who had wanted him to go into law. "All as he wanted you to do, was to do something with your life," she would say to him. Her biggest disappointment was her daughter Vera, and she did not want Ralphie to be a Vera!

"You know, Ralphie, that it isn't any kind of life to hang around downtown – that can only lead to trouble. We have one girl now who does that. We have one girl who didn't even come to his funeral. We have one girl already, Ralphie, who travels about with hippie people and has lived in a commune and was married and divorced. We have one girl now, Ralphie, like that – "

Then she would look at him, breathe deeply, and return her gaze to the far side of the den.

Sometimes he would go and visit his mother and bring Adele along with him. Her house was beyond the tracks, above Myhrra's trailer, and it would loom up sorrowfully in the night air. There was a stream that ran through some dying bushes behind it, and an old swing sat in the trampled grass. The fence boards were loose and rattled in the wind, the brick made the windows look blank, and though the front yard had been landscaped, there was an unfinished quality to it. The garage was huge and smelled of chipped paint. Adele and he would sit out on the swing, which was hidden from the wind, and sometimes you could see her unbuttoned coat flapping. There was a smell of iron in the autumn evening, the pervading scent of apples in the darkening lanes.

Beyond the swing, on the other side of the shed, which was brand new and had nothing in it but a lawn hose, beyond the trampled garden, too, there was a small enclosure where they used to go after school to get away from everyone. Adele would sit on Ralphie's knee and eat carrots – which she constantly did for her eyes because she was afraid of going blind. Ralphie would put his hands up under her coat, and down the top of her elastic pants to keep them warm, and Adele, tapping her feet and chewing carrots, would worry about her teeth going bad and her eyes getting strained from looking at the blackboard. There would be wind along her legs, and the smell of frost in the upturned earth, earth that had amongst the stones the hardness of turnips.

7

Joe Walsh started working when he was fourteen. He joined the navy just after his seventeenth birthday, and was a diver on the HMCS *Yukon*. One time, because of a remark made by the Chief Petty Officer about someone Joe knew, Joe threw him down the teak-wood stairs leading to the galley. He was sent off to jail because of this. The Chief Petty Officer said it was an unprovoked attack, and Joe, stubborn – and with a trait that men often have, who believe that if they are stubborn they are right – refused to speak or to defend himself. He then got fed up with the navy and came home. He married Rita, while all of those that knew her wondered why she would bother with him. They had two children.

It was in his nature to drink, and he had to drink – he wouldn't be himself if he didn't. To be what he was – what image he had of himself – it was only natural and authentic that he do so.

He crossed the line after he was thirty, that is, he fell under a tractor while fighting a fire. He was laid up for almost a year – periodically. And finally lost his job, and got drunk every day. Every time he drank, Joe would resolve to quit. Sitting about the tavern, or down at the wharf, or working outside around the house, or hobbling once again to the liquor store through a variety of streets, as if he was making for himself some obstacle course and really wasn't thinking of the wine he was about to buy, he would resolve to quit.

He would take his bottles down to the bank and throw them over – only to climb down after them in the middle of the night. The bank was about sixty yards from their back door, which faced the river. There were small spaces of grass and alders where men and women hid away in the afternoons to drink – old veterans and girls who had grown up to go nowhere, and ended up at fifty somehow still in print dresses, their hair clasped by some silver broach. Joe often hopped down there to drink with them, and they would sing some songs together. And sometimes one of his friends, a salesman from the Gaspé, who always had a bottle in the trunk of his car, would come along. Joe would bring him into the house, and the man would try to get Adele to call him Uncle Pete. Then in the morning Joe wouldn't be able to stare himself or anyone else in the face. He would sit out in the porch, with his chair turned about facing the wall, while Rita and Adele walked out the door to church.

Once in January in his bare feet, he walked down over the bank and stepped on a broken wine bottle, cutting through to a tendon. After this his left foot bothered him also, and he found that he could no longer get a job full time – but only part-time doing odd jobs. For a while he took a job with a local finance company repossessing furniture. He would go into houses and while children cried in bewilderment and men swore at him and threatened him, and women both yelled and pleaded, outside the days were bright, and the heat played down like a vapour on the steps, and dandelion heads lay tousled in the fresh-mown grass. He would take away chairs and couches – and feel sick of himself and the world. After a while he gave almost everything up, except drink.

Because of his difficulty, Rita had to start fending for herself at a time when it wasn't as accepted or as natural for women to go out to work. At this time, for a woman to work meant the family had somehow fallen. That is, the very women who today were saying that a woman's career was indispensable were quite prepared to stay home then, because staying home was as much commonplace as working now is. But Rita, and a thousand Rita's like her, worked every day.

Joe remained in this phase of his drinking for seven years. Pledges from the priest didn't solve matters, even when Father Dolan walked in telling Joe he would go to hell – if hell was not where he already was – while Rita sat in the corner, her breasts heavy, and Joe, who towered over the priest, nodded like a child.

Joe managed to stay away from the hospitals and clinics, and managed to stay clear of anyone who suggested they might have a solution for his drinking. In those days he hated the AA and the detox with a passion, and cursed every time they were mentioned. He also looked at Rita at this time as if he was blaming her for something that no one else understood.

Some nights they would find him alongside the ditch, as far away as Ridge Road, with his coat and mittens on, alone in a snowbank. Adele became coolly efficient at spotting his huge somewhat misshapen back against the long evening sky.

Then he gave it up for three months.

One night, after that three months, when Rita needed him to baby-sit, his nerves were bad; that is, she was going

61

out with people he felt had made fun of him and he felt one drink would make everything all right.

Well, all I need is one drink, he thought to himself. *One beer. What's a beer – it is nothing – a beer is nothing – it's not going to be like last time – yes last time – "*

And with these thoughts he went back and forth and looked out the window nervously – convinced at this instant that he would not drink. Or if he did everything would be different.

He had promised Rita he would baby-sit Adele. Rita was helping to make props for the Christmas play, she was pregnant with Milly. She had tried to get Joe interested in the Christmas play because she knew as long as he was working he would not drink – and Rita perhaps could also sense a drunk coming on.

It was getting close to Christmas and Joe had always found staying sober at Christmas impossible.

"Keep care of Delly – I'll keep care of Delly – no problem."

Thinking of a drink he was accustomed to the immediate fear that was now associated with this thought – and then the overwhelming security that he had been dry for three months – and that one beer wouldn't hurt.

One beer is not going to make the difference between life and death, he thought. The fact that Rita did housework for people who had no respect for him suddenly came to mind and made him angry.

He woke up Adele and put her in the half-ton and headed to the tavern. He had stolen the Christmas money that Rita kept in the kitchen drawer, but he only planned to use a small amount of it, and he proceeded to buy two draft, while Adele waited out in the truck. He stared at them for an hour – almost, he was sure – resolved to not drink them.

Later that night he made it back home – up over the bank with stars sparkling off the snow, singing an old Irish song he'd learned on his ship, remembering a fight in Vancouver, and forgetting completely about the truck, or Adele sitting in it.

Rita was still a young woman and there were men, who for obvious reasons thought she was easy, or available. That is, they *assumed* concern for her, because they could condescend to her husband. To make matters worse, they often pretended that they liked Joe, and that they wished to include him in what they did. Joe would sometimes find himself going somewhere with Rita, and feeling that she was embarrassed he was there.

Joe felt, only rightly, that it was not him they wanted, it was her, and though he didn't tell Rita this, the same stubbornness he had when he had thrown the Chief Petty Officer down the stairs came over him.

8

As it happened, every six or seven months Myhrra would find new friends. And so, caught up with new friends, Myhrra didn't come to the house very often. Sometimes, feeling obligated, she would drop in, sit down in the chair for a moment, and then she would be out the door after a cup of tea.

One always knows how a family feels toward you by how the children react to your presence. It was invariable that Adele and Milly were now scared stiff that Myhrra would leave once she got there, or that she would stay only a certain amount of time, or that Joe or Rita, who seemed to have no one coming in at all anymore, would do something to make her leave. Adele would always try to tell some jokes to lighten everyone up, and Milly would tell these jokes right after her. Myhrra would sit there listening, in her blue slacks and kerchief, and then, just at the punch line (or so it seemed to Adele), she would get ready to leave. No matter how fast she told her joke, or no matter what style she told it in, or no matter how Rita sat, Myhrra would (it seemed to Adele) be unable to get the punch line.

The whole family felt they had done something wrong.

One night Adele saw a group of cars in Myhrra's yard.

"Go on up, go on up," Adele said to Rita, excitedly. "I'll baby-sit, I will I will. Go on up, they're probably playing auction or something."

"I'll behave – I'll behave," Milly screeched, running about the house. "I'll behave – "

Rita got dressed and went out, only to come back a few minutes later. When Adele pestered her she got angry.

"They're having a bridge party up there," she said. "I'm not going to intrude on a bunch of ladies sitting down to play a game of bridge. I have a load of ironing to do as it is."

"Ha, you could beat any of them," Adele screamed, throwing a sudden tantrum and throwing a dishcloth over Milly's head, and then kicking a chair.

"I haven't played bridge in my life," Rita said.

And then for some reason Adele got doubly angry at this.

Rita, with her loose top and her ponytail and her scuffed shoes, smiled and asked Adele and Milly to help her make divinity fudge, but Adele went upstairs instead and played an old Beatles record, while Milly stood at her door begging her to come out.

It was a tradition for Myhrra to take Adele for a drive on Tuesday afternoons. On one particular day Myhrra was quieter than usual, and Adele, sitting on the passenger side of the car and staring out the window at the river, past houses and fields, tried desperately to think of something nice to say, but every time Myhrra glanced at her she would promptly look at her boots.

Myhrra stopped on a lane and looked at the field with some apple trees in it. She got out of the car and stayed outside for a long time, leaning against the hood and staring, smoking one cigarette after another. It was the field that she and Mike, her ex-husband, had at one time owned, and which they sold during their divorce.

"Do you want me to come outside, My?" Adele said, rolling down the window half an inch. "What are you thinking about?"

"H'm?"

"What are you thinking?"

"Nothing so much."

"I have to pee, My."

"Pardon me?"

"I have to real bad. My back teeth are floating about, the school bus has already gone down river."

"I know, I know, Delly dear. Just a moment, I have to pee too."

Another few minutes went by and Myhrra stayed exactly where she was, with the red kerchief she wore blowing up in a gust of autumn wind, and the smell of pebbles.

"I was invited to your house for supper tonight, Delly hon, but I can't go. Tell your mom I'll see her tomorrow."

Adele looked at the big rabbit paw on the mirror and stroked it for good luck.

Myhrra didn't visit them for some time, spending more time with her friends from across the river. One night just after Rita had closed the drapes, they heard Myhrra's car turn in their yard, and blow the horn, but no one this time went to the window.

Myhrra still made it to the hospital every Wednesday. One day a voice called out to her as she passed a room.

"Hey!" he said. The voice belonged to Allain Garret. He was an old man from down river who worked in the woods. He had seven daughters and five sons, worked cutting pulp, and had a huge television in the centre of his living room, with one family chair. The floor was brown tiled and a thousand hockey games were watched from this chair. During the 1972 series with Russia, he had taken off the front door so his friends could sit in the porch and watch it. But because so many people stopped in at the house to watch it, he was himself pushed to the background, and ended up watching it, leaning through one of the porch windows, while people half stood and half crouched in front of him, and his nieces and nephews sat on the stairs. One of his little nieces, Gidget, who was eight at the time with big brown eyes, leaned on his shoulder and went to sleep in the sun. When Canada scored the winning goal, he happened to be staring at a potted plant that his wife had left on the sill, and he was thinking of its green stem, and how that reminded him of the sea. It was only a momentary reflection, but he missed the goal.

Myhrra went in, and there was a smell to the large room of white sheets and the faint scent of blood. There were six beds in the room but only three patients. Allain Garret had cut his stomach open falling against a stake, and now happily showed her the wound. Myhrra looked at it unpleasantly, and tied her kerchief tighter. His skin was brown, and scarred, his fingers were bent in all different directions. Joe Walsh was sitting in the corner talking to him.

"Here's Myhrra – " Allain said, smiling, and trying to reach some candy on the bedside table to give to her.

There is always something frightening in the human body when it is incapacitated. His hands were rough and his elbows looked thin, as if he was now losing his strength. Myhrra at this moment stood very still and could not bring herself to look at Joe. Myhrra very quietly asked to see his wound again – for some reason she thought she should do this. She kept staring straight ahead.

"Well, you should take care of yourself," she said, suddenly, in an unnatural voice.

Allain then offered her some more candy, which she hadn't taken the first time. Then she tried to think of the names of his sons and daughters to ask him about. Unfortunately she forgot that Claude was in prison, and this was the only name she could think of.

"Where is Claude now?" Myhrra asked, in a loud, somewhat angry voice.

"Claude's fine," Allain said. "Still in jail." He smiled, and then suddenly made fun of himself and his injury. Then he made fun of Joe not drinking any more, which was done in a totally harmless way, but Myhrra stared straight ahead, blinking, as if there was nothing in Joe they could possibly find funny.

Allain again turned on Joe and said that he shouldn't be so foolish. And then he commented on the time Myhrra had pulled her dress up over her head, one evening in the summer long ago, to show the flowers on her brassiere, when she was thirteen. Then at this moment Joe felt that he should not laugh at this. So old Allain did not know what to do, except look about here and there and comment on things, and ask no one in particular if it was snowing outside.

Finally he looked embarrassed because the visit had become as painful to him as to everyone else.

9

Joe got home from visiting Allain Garret to find that Adele had been caught shoplifting. Rita was at the kitchen table and Milly was watching television. She had five or six dolls sitting on the couch with her, and her great big rainbow-coloured hat on. She was in her nightgown, had no panties on, and was sitting there with her mother's three big blue brushes, brushing the dolls' hair.

The grass was covered in snow, but there were still patches of it bare. The house was on a slope, with the driveway pointed down to some alders. Joe went outside to carry the garbage cans to the street, and when he did, he could see Adele's bedroom light – it was covered with an orange peel to make the room glow. Sometimes during Joe's drinking days he would see that light burning at two or two-thirty in the morning as he came home through the old back lot, stumbling over the rocks. As soon as he would get halfway across the lot, he would see the light go out. It never failed. He stood outside for a moment thinking. He huffed and spit and lit a cigarette. He could see ice on the porch steps, and it glistened under the faint porch light. He rubbed his face for a second and went back inside. The whole house was occupied by his family and the huge philodendron that sat over by the wall.

Before going home, Allain had asked him to go down river and see to it that his chickens and pigs were being fed, and asked him to see to it that some rocks were put into the pig troughs, for the pigs to chew on, and asked him to go into the woods on their land and check his wood lot. He was sure he would get out of the hospital any day, but things had to get done and he couldn't rely on his son who was home, who never went outside in the winter, unless it was to pick up his mail.

So he asked Joe to do it, and Joe complied. It was easy enough to check the wood lot, to see that the wood Allain had yarded was still there, and Joe walked down to the brook to check for any deer signs. It was a cold afternoon, and there was a breeze at the top of the trees. Just a few months ago, he and Rita had come here to fish for trout, and now everything was cold and bleak. But the coldness and bleakness gave Joe a thrill because it smelled of hunting. And he could actually scent the deer, and know they were here.

At dusk the sky took on a reddish haze over the trees. When Joe was a youngster he used to work with his father out here. He would not get to town very often, but sometimes he would hitchhike alone up to a dance. He would walk up the street just at dusk, when the convent was lighted, and the courthouse steps looked solitary, and there was a sting in his legs because of the cold. Sometimes, when he couldn't get a lift, he would hike home; and so, sometimes late, with the smell of hides and animals coming to the road, he would make his way, a silent lonely light flicking far out on the bay.

Joe sat under a rotted stand for a while, near the brook. He wondered why he had not died that time he got caught up in a turbine in the Bay of Fundy. He was thinking of this as he sat there.

He had felt his way along the round turbine for ten minutes, and found that he had not progressed in the right direction. In fact he had to swim back, but he had to swim back as carefully as he had come, or else lose his sense of direction completely.

Yes, it was all so strange. If anyone asked him what had happened he wouldn't be able to tell them. Halfway back along the wall he had to switch to his reserve tank. And he finally found his way through the opening and back to the surface, with four minutes of air left.

For some reason he felt that he had something more to do, and every time he did something he felt that wasn't it. He shuddered suddenly and spit through his legs. Milly needed new pills because she was hyperactive and they were going to put her on Ritalin. Last spring she went sliding and fell over the embankment behind the house, and he carried her home. The next afternoon, she climbed out the window and tried to get onto the roof. Then she got caught in a pipe under the street, and everyone could hear someone whistling and yelling underneath the pavement, and it so happened it was Milly, stuck in a little drain-pipe.

He thought of this for a moment. He thought of the turbine, and how he had managed to get into it without knowing that he was – and then how did he manage to get out of it?

While he sat there the sky smelled of ash and darkness. There was always a feeling of hunger. He straightened one leg out, to relax it. Off in the undergrowth he heard a snap, and saw a buck tine glimmer in a space of light between two heavy trees. Then it was gone.

*

When he got home, Rita, furious with Adele and her shop-lifting, told Joe to go upstairs and "shake the living shit out of your daughter."

Milly looked at him and said:

"Hi Daddy – you gonna go get her?"

"Sure I am."

He sat down heavily on the couch beside Milly and picked up a doll. He smiled at her and kissed her doll and then she got him to kiss all of her other dolls. Then she kissed him and asked to feel the bump on his back.

Then he picked her up and took her upstairs to bed.

After he put Milly to bed he went in to see Adele. It was the second time she had been caught shoplifting. The first time, she had only stolen some eye shadow, but this time she had shoved five packages of panty-hose down her pants, and was caught trying to walk sideways out of the store.

"Zellers wasn't made to keep the likes of you in panty-hose," Joe said, coming into the room, and looking about gruffly. Her room had been completely changed over since he had last been in it. Now there was a big poster of a flower above her bed, when before there wasn't. Now there was a sign on her door saying: "To all little creeps – stay out on pain of death," whereas before there wasn't. Also her bras and beanies were lying about the room, and her pant-ies were lying on the chair. Joe noticed all of this quickly and felt he had intruded. He stepped over to the chair and moved the panties off carefully. He sat down.

Adele was lying in bed reading. Her face was white, and her lips moved over what she read. Now and then she slapped the magazine pages abruptly. The Russian ship whistle sounded in the distance. There was a great big curler in her hair, right at the top, while her hair was taped down on the sides, which made her ears look particularly innocent.

"How come you didn't visit old Allain – ya know," he stuttered. "We been down there for supper a hunnred times?"

"As no relation to me," Adele said, under her breath.

"Ya used ta get him ta buy bubblegum for your hockey cards though, didn't ya?" he said. "Ole Allain walkin around chewin big wads of bubblegum." Adele sniffed.

Her pink blouse was buttoned up to her throat and made her skin look cream-coloured, except for a little pimple on her nose, which had a dab of Noxzema on it.

Joe had a stutter and Adele liked to mimic it when she was showing off. So he was often hesitant to speak to her in case she would start to mimic his stutter. Sometimes when he was out in the woods alone, he would go up to a tree and say: "Hello how are you, me name's Joe Walsh, boiler-maker, mechanic of sorts who lives with Rita and two kids," and would not stutter at all, and nod with conviction.

And it seemed as if he would be able to pronounce every word correctly from that moment forward, and that he would never stutter again. But by the time he got home, the same identifiable stoppage in speech would have reappeared.

Even Rita became intolerant and impatiently finished sentences for him. Adele had picked up on this also and she would finish sentences that he hadn't even intended to say.

The stutter only came when he was nervous, as he was

when he went to the unemployment centre to talk about getting a job, or now and then when he went out with Rita to a play at the high school or church.

Joe sat in a chair with a cigarette in his hand. His bottom lip had puffed out and had developed a little sack for putting snuff. He sat on his fingers and looked about. On the dresser, there was an old black and white picture of Adele as a child with pigeons all over her body. Her arms and legs were covered with pigeons, and two pigeons were sitting on her head, and she had the absurdest look of terror on her face. Seeing this and Adele's pictures of flowers, and her decals and stickers, Joe, sitting there with his large arms and shoulders, once again felt as if he had intruded and that there was no way he could be stern with her. He had every intention of being stern when he came into the room, but now he became silent, and listened to the train off in the distance above the creamery.

And suddenly without knowing he was going to, he told her he had not meant to hurt them when he was drinking, and he was sorry she had melancholy feelings.

He spoke about his last drinking binge which lasted eighteen days. Days went by and he wanted to come home, but he couldn't bring himself to. He thought everyone would have gone. At one point he woke up sitting in this office. Everyone was walking back and forth and not paying the slightest bit of attention to him. The personnel manager was standing over in the corner whispering to the secretary, who was looking at him. Joe found out that he was in a mine in Quebec. How he'd gotten there he didn't know, except it seemed perfectly obvious he should be there.

They had sent for a guard because they didn't speak English well and he didn't speak French. He finally made it clear that he was going to send for his family and bring

74

them all to Quebec, and with that resolved, he started on his way again.

As always, he found a tavern and forgot all about going to Quebec. Two days later he was in Truro, Nova Scotia, drinking with people who had become his friends, and who were all going to come and visit him. He remembered then that he had promised himself he would never drink again. He had had all the will in the world to stop. He had even started his own business, of auto body repair, and he had had cards printed, and even had taken out ads on the radio. But though again, as always, and like many drunks, he was capable of making money quite handily, he got drunk. And once he was drinking, whatever he had been doing seemed all wrong and all worthless, and something else had to be done, something which was different from anything he had ever done before.

Next he found himself in jail in Richibucto. And after a day on the road, with seventeen beer to sober himself up, he found himself sitting in a chair in the kitchen with Adele trying to feed him soup.

As he told her this story, Adele said nothing. Now and then she would sniff, as if she wasn't listening, and turn a page of her magazine.

"Now I know it's a disease," he said hopefully, almost to himself. "I never knew that before."

He looked at his hands, and rubbed them together, and then looked at the picture she had of Ralphie sitting on her night table.

The curler on her head made her look as if she had a unicorn horn just above her forehead.

Then Joe told her that he drank when he was young, but that maybe he couldn't drink anymore, and was going to do his best not to drink again. But that didn't mean they would ever be rich. He smiled clumsily. He said he remembered a lot more than she might think – yes, he did. He remembered when they lived downtown, and there was no heat in the apartment, and Adele got colds. He remembered that. And Rita almost lost Milly, and the social workers came and were going to take away the children. He remembered that. He remembered how Adele used to carry soup cans about in her dress pockets, and a big can opener, because she thought that's what was needed to cure his hangover, and she would hand it up to him when he came home – and that one time she kept a doll he'd won for her at the circus under her pillow. He bet she didn't remember that. He smiled and looked about, and then coughed. And then suddenly without even knowing he was going to do it, he asked her to forgive him.

"I see," she said, as he spoke. "I see."

She glanced at him quickly and her eyes got round, and then she glanced back at her book.

"I see," she said. "Yes, of course – I see."

10

The Russian ship *Gorki* had been stranded here for three weeks. A Petty Officer, Terrisov, became friendly with Myhrra. And she showed him about the river, took him to the curling club, and explained the rules of the game to him, and for a time seemed to forget her problems.

There were tours of the Russian ship organized, and times allotted for the Russians to go skating. The ship was being repaired, and for a time it was only natural to be friendly to stranded foreigners until they left. For some reason, at this time Ralphie became friendly with Terrisov as well. They discussed hockey and boxing, professional versus amateur sport, and complimented each other on their respective teams. One afternoon when Myhrra was with them, Myhrra said someone had told her that the Russians were superior in hockey, and in sports in general. She looked at Ralphie and sighed deeply, as if she was now tired of most Canadians.

Terrisov diplomatically said that though the Canadians were great hockey players, what bothered him was that they refused to put *fun* in their sport. They would undoubtedly benefit from training harder and earning less money.

He neglected to mention the 1972 series. It was not mentioned by Terrisov, and Myhrra knew nothing about it. She only nodded her head as if she had finally found someone who agreed with her. Ralphie, listening more than he spoke, felt overall that Terrisov was acting something like an older brother to them, and therefore could be much harsher to them than he was.

There were certain things that Terrisov could not get away from and one was the curfew put upon the men on the ship. The curfew was for eight o'clock and any visitors to the ship went on organized tours during the afternoon. Byron and Myhrra were continually down near the ship or on the wharf.

During one of these tours Byron happened to be caught picking up some loose Russian cigarettes and putting them into his pocket.

The Russian he took them from noticed and spoke in Russian to Terrisov. Terrisov took them out of Byron's pocket. The other Russian went away speaking to himself. Byron looked at Myhrra and began to yell at her. Terrisov contemplated something a moment, his shoulders thrust back, and as little Milly grinned, Terrisov who saw the grin, suddenly said:

"This is not done here – anything you want, you ask. We don't have thieves here."

Then he looked at Myhrra, who blushed, and then he picked up Milly, who was still grinning, and continued on.

There was a feeling that they shouldn't do anything to hurt the Russians' feelings, because the Russians were innocent – innocent, abrupt, and overbearing – a feeling that Ralphie had. Whenever he spoke to Terrisov he thought instinctively: *They will never admit a fault to us – therefore we don't want to offend them.*

This was what happened to the bridge. The ship had

drifted with the current and hit the span, creating a bulk along the underside of the bridge and causing a million dollars' worth of damage. The Russians were silent for days and then they made a statement about it. It was the Norwegian ship's fault, the ship with the load of telephone poles had not moved out of the channel properly, or at the right time, and to avoid hitting it on the port side they had shut their engines, and had drifted with the tide waters – it was the only thing they could do – and they hit the bridge. It was lucky no one was injured but the other ship was already out to sea, and what could be done? They had made out their report to the harbour master and were now preparing to leave. Restitution? No! It would not be proper for them to pay.

This idea that it would not be proper fascinated Ralphie. What was supposedly proper and what wasn't was a part of their make up more than any other sailors Ralphie had ever met.

Adele said she did not like them ever since the 1972 hockey series. She saw how some of her friends – and some radio and television commentators – started to lose heart in the Canadian team, and even took to ridiculing it. At her young age, she did not understand that criticism of your own in Canada was often considered fashionable expertise. It was her and Joe's favourite game – one which she still watched every Saturday night – she could never understand the criticisms that were levelled against it. Adele told Ralphie that she had to stay in the bathroom throwing up during much of the games, and when the Canadians lost a game she would go about the house like a ghost refusing to eat, and prayed, her lips moving slowly: "Oh God – let Pete Mahovlich get a goal."

Nor could she read the reports in the paper about it, or listen to the radio – because, to her, so many of the reports seemed wrong. There was hardly a thing about September 1972 that she remembered, except that we played eight hockey games against the Russians, which we won – and she met Ralphie Pillar for the first time.

For Adele who had always loved hockey, and especially the Montreal Canadiens, this 1972 series between the Canadians and the Russians, was the one spiritual happening she could think of. It might have seemed silly to a few, but the greater majority of Canadians thought like she did. And she felt betrayed by anyone who happened to downplay the event in any way. Especially when those who didn't know what it signified downplayed it to show *their* level of expertise and fair play.

Adele with her feet thrust back and her toes wiggling would make up names for Russian hockey players while Ralphie went around the apartment.

"How about," Adele would say, with her innocent complexion and a spot on her nose, "Alexi Snipmyweineroff. Or," she would continue mischievously, "Symka Feelmyarseoff." Then she would look at Ralphie through her eyelashes and grin. "As long as you are going to add 'off,' Ralphie, you can get a pretty good Russian name, like, 'It's Feelmearseoff who passes over to Snipmeweineroff, back to Blowmeholeoff.'" And with this, she would sit there, wiggling her toes.

And after a suitable pause she would say: "Seaman Rotchercockoff."

Once Myhrra went to the ship alone. It was at night. There was oil on the water, and the wind was blowing heavily. She could smell tar, and her hair blew against the left side of her face. She went down to the ship using the old path, crossed the ditch with its ice, and the road. Some sharp snow hit her eyes and they watered. The ship's lights cast a glow over the front streets of town.

The ship was ready to go the next day and Terrisov was expecting her. But she felt uncomfortable. She had been to the ship for the last two weeks and now felt foolish. For some reason, she did not know there would be women and children on the ship – and Terrisov, once she got there, seemed indifferent toward her, and even indignant about something. Tonight, one woman kept looking at her, as if she assumed she knew all about her and Myhrra was guilty of something. Myhrra's platinum blonde hair, which was wet and looked darker, and her large round earrings – which she had put on because she thought they made her look good – now felt ugly.

One of the women wanted to protect Terrisov from her – probably she thought for his own good – and Terrisov, who might have once thought it was a great idea to have a woman come aboard, was now nervous. He showed her a picture of a small town outside of Leningrad, and talked about his wife who was studying engineering. Then he looked at Myhrra, and for some reason, with her dyed hair and blue slacks, which were carefully upturned at the cuffs, and the zipper of her pants, which seemed to protrude as if she had a paunch, she felt belittled. It had been a long time since she had felt this way. She sat on a chair in his room and looked at him, and smiled and looked about when he said anything. Two men came by, and they stood in the doorway, and she smiled, and they stood there for a few moments watching her. Then one man went, and another man came. He said something in Russian, and the first man grinned, and then their shoulders shrugged as Terrisov said something to them which sounded unpleasant.

81

There was a chess game going on and Terrisov took her to watch it. She didn't know anything about chess. The room was crowded with people, and when she turned about, the same woman who wanted to protect Terrisov from her was staring straight at her, and Myhrra became frightened. Once when Terrisov said something to her she laughed loudly and coarsely – but only because she laughed that way when she was nervous.

Then they went back along the galleyway, passed some doors to Terrisov's room, and she sat back down. His whole neck and face were red, and for some time he kept looking about, as if he didn't want to put his eyes on her. Her whole dressing up and getting ready seemed terrible at this moment.

It was all so different from how she thought it would be, and all so different than he himself had led himself to believe it would be.

She lit a cigarette, which she held in the sort of affectation of sophistication she had learned from childhood until this moment, and she, too, began to talk. She spoke of her ex-husband Mike, and how she was sorry for him, and how he was getting married to this young girl – and how she was going to go to the girl and warn her all about Mike the next day. (Myhrra said she was going to do this although she knew in her heart she wasn't.) And she gossiped about her friends. She told him she couldn't get anywhere in a town like this and the whole river was just as bad. Then with that affectation of sophistication that she had learned from childhood, she smiled, and butted her cigarette carefully.

"Ah what a sad person you are," Terrisov said, because, quite by chance, he realized as she spoke that he would have an opportunity to say this – and the line, for some dumb reason, stuck in his head. The little woman with the shiny black hair passed and looked at them just as Terrisov spoke, and it sounded as if he was lecturing her. Then Terrisov quite suddenly looked out the doorway and waved at her, joyously, as if to let her know he too understood some sort of reprimand toward Myhrra was needed.

11

Joe got up at five every morning. He would look out the window, wonder what type of day it was going to be, smoke a cigarette, and then go downstairs and put on the kettle. Then he would go about town playing punch-boards and sit in the malls.

Each day Joe would go downtown and see how people were doing. Then he would go to the unemployment office to see if there were any jobs. Then, on those days Rita was out, he would come back and do the housework, make lunch, and then go back downtown again. Sometimes he would stand about the corner listening to men talk, and then he would go up the hill once more, walk along the highway, and back to his house, where he would peel potatoes and wait for Adele.

Adele would come into the house, look at a bit of dust on the table or a piece of bread with some gnaw marks in it left by Milly and look very sceptically at him. Then she would smile slightly and go up to her room, put on her Led Zeppelin album, and call Ralphie.

Ralphie would show up, and help Joe and Milly find her skates. Every day Milly would lose her skates, and would have every pot and kettle and mitt and sock on the kitchen floor, looking for them. Then after they found her skates, away they would go to the skating rink.

Joe would tie Milly's skates, and lift her over the boards and watch her go. She would go like a dynamo around the rink three or four times on her ankles, yelling and screaming and falling down, and then they would head off home again.

By the time they got home, Rita would have supper ready and Adele would have already disappeared downtown with Cindi. They would all have supper; Rita would get ready and go curling, which she had started to do this fall, and Joe would do the dishes and wait for Adele to come home. Usually he had a meeting at eight o'clock and Adele would make it in anywhere from ten to eight until ten after.

She would come in and he would be able to tell immediately how she was faring with her new friend. She would walk in without giving him a chance to speak and would say: "Well are you going to your meeting or not?"

"Yes."

"Well go," she would say. "Go to your funny meeting."

He would go to his meeting. Generally he sat along the left side of the hall at a table with two or three other men. Joe did not know why this simple meeting of forty or fifty men and women alcoholics would keep him from drinking for another day. He only knew it to be true.

There were some people there, however, whom Joe did not like, and could only try to like. A very few who had gotten sober talked about having money now. When they spoke Joe would often fidget or look about discontentedly. But he found out that the other men and women put up with them and didn't seem to mind, so he should not mind either.

At first one of these men, Henry, had promised Joe a job. Now, though, he had seemed to have forgotten all about it. Every time he saw Joe, Henry smiled and patted him on the back and asked him how he was doing and Joe would nod. "That's good, that's good – you come to the round up this month and bring your wife," the man would say.

Henry wore a toupee, and since it was ill-fitting, it made his forehead look unusually wide and the top of his head looked like it had two different types of hair. The man was completely unconcerned that this made him look funny, and didn't care if it made him look better or worse. When he walked in front of you, the first thing you looked at was the top of his head.

He would always be laughing, his toupee just off centre, which, because it was off centre, suddenly made you notice his false teeth. He had not had a drink in five years. He had no stomach because he had drunk it away. He had almost bled to death twice. He had taken fifteen thousand dollars to the bank for his accounting company, and then had drawn out the whole thing and gone away with his girlfriend. Then he had come home, run the car off the road, and had scalped himself. It was the last drunk he had been on.

Now, sitting here in this room, with its smell of smoke, he kept telling Joe that he was content that he had gone through all of this.

"What do you mean?" Joe would ask hesitantly.

"You don't stutter in here as much as you do outside," the man would say, patting Joe on the back and laughing loudly.

Joe, at first, was furious with this. Why would anyone say those things to him. His initial reaction was that he had made a mistake, that this sobriety business was foolish, and he would have nothing to do with it. He would go out and get drunk. But something kept making him come back.

He also found that there were men who had drunk far more than he did, who were much tougher, who had lost much more, and now not only did not drink anymore but looked at everyone in simple kindness.

But Henry took a special interest in him. In fact he never left him alone, and Joe got used to him being there. This was the man who bothered Joe, and whom Joe disliked, and yet it was to this man Joe wanted to prove more than anyone else that he could stop drinking.

Every time Joe thought of taking a drink that first little while, he thought of that man with the brown toupee, and he would say: "If he can stay sober, so can I."

12

After a while, Ruby and Janet tired of Adele and stopped going to the apartment. Adele would meet them on the street.

"Hey girls – there's beer at Ralphie's," she would say. "He bought it for you."

She would try to say it in exactly the same way that two months ago would have them all hugging her and walking arm in arm with her (hugging was very important amongst these girls). However it didn't matter now how she said it.

"Well, Delly, we have things to do," Janet would say.

"My name's not Delly, it's Adele," she would whisper, though she was suddenly frightened of them. They all laughed as if this had always been *the joke* – and this was the one irreverent joke that they had always held dear and one that she knew nothing about. Even little Cindi, who was always taking fits, and whose mouth was too wide, and whose father tried to get in her pants, laughed with her faint eyelashes closed, catching the snow on them.

Janet, who talked in a sort of whispering shriek and who always wore a pleated skirt, with nylons, and a birthmark on her knee, her ears sticking out from her combed hair like two half-moons, said: "Oh why don't you tell us some stories about your sick father and family."

"I don't have a sick father and family," Adele said. Her mouth was a pencil line. "I have a good family."

"Not the way you talk," Ruby said, as if this again was the major point in everything that had passed between them these last two months, even though these stories were told with the idea that she was becoming part of the group when she told them, and was doing everything everyone else did.

"Cindi," Adele said, blinking under her knitted hat while snow fell upon it in the dark.

"Don't Cindi her," Ruby said. "Ya always made fun of her as being a fit-taker."

"I – I never did," Adele said.

Cindi suddenly looked reflective because she was being talked about. "An epileptic," she whispered.

Ruby smiled, her teeth white in the cold air outside the store. More than Janet, she had always unnerved Adele because Adele was in love with her and everything she did.

They looked at her – they were all standing near Zellers and people were coming and going through the doors – old men were walking by, and ladies in snow boots, with their perfume smelling of wet fall snow. Across the street Myhrra was looking out the beauty shop window at them, her nose pressed into the pane. Adele was sweating under her arms, as always whenever she got nervous, and yet the cold blew on her face and made her dizzy. There was a smell of lights and fish and chips.

"You've said too much already," Ruby said. "About us – god knows what you said about us – called us a bunch a whores and said we screw boys and talked behind our backs and everything else – "

Cindi sighed and looked about. On her back was a great big peace sign, printed with red magic marker, and she had drawn two of them on her knees as well, so when she walked the first thing you saw coming towards you was two peace signs.

After a moment they turned and walked away, leaving Adele standing there.

13

It was just about this time that Ralphie's sister came back home. Her name was Vera. She was about twenty-five. It was 1973 and Ralphie had not seen her in four years.

Vera was tall and thin, and she wore a pair of granny glasses with golden frames and big long flowery dresses. Vera often came into the apartment and sat down on the beanbag chair they had in the corner, listening to a conversation. After the conversation went on for a certain amount of time she would get up and leave, walking away in silence with her boyfriend Nevin, age thirty-two, following her, wearing his flowered shirt, medallion, and bell-bottom pants.

Vera would stare at Adele, and after a while Adele, without knowing that she was doing it, found herself sitting exactly the same way as Vera, and speaking in the same tone of voice, although Vera had affected a sort of British accent from a year at Oxford that Adele could not muster.

As a little girl Vera had read all of Jane Austin. She began writing poems, and they had a poetry group at noon hour in the school. She was interested in all kinds of things. (Nevin hadn't read anything but because he grew a beard everyone assumed he had.) Vera always seemed to be alone. Ralphie would watch her coming up the lane, as a schoolgirl carrying her books in her arms, with her big round glasses fogged up and snow falling on her hair. Because she always ate oranges the boys used to call her sucker. And she was always looking for new friends. And there was a great deal of silence about her. Once she had a pen pal, but then after a while the letters stopped coming. Vera would walk down to the post office to make sure there was not some mistake, but finally after about ten months realized that she wasn't going to get a letter again.

She stayed at home. She never went out anywhere. Sometimes her father would get angry with her and tease her about being a stick in the mud. He would walk by her and shout out "Stick in the muck," and she would be stubborn enough to stay in days at a time because of this. For a while, because Ralphie was doing science projects, she gave up writing poetry and began to study biology. Then she would come home and talk about reproduction – which embarrassed Thelma. Then Vera became very clinically minded about reproduction. It was reproduction this, and reproduction that. She had a Bristol board where she put United Nations speeches. And she wrote an essay on selling wheat to China, which won a prize. She thought for a while she was going to go to the United Nations, but she never got to go. Ralphie at that time, and still, had a tremendous affection for her – they once built a fort in the gully together – but at the same time he felt she would not or could not be close to him.

"I'm not like I used to be, am I, Ralph?" she sometimes asked, while she sat in his apartment.

"No," Ralphie would say, scratching his ears and blushing.

"Why are you blushing then?"

"I'm not."

"I suppose you are the same old person you always were, Ralphie." She would look at him over the top of her glasses and smile so quickly, and then frown right after it, that Ralphie was never sure whether he'd seen a smile or not.

"I don't know," Ralphie would say grinning, and looking confused.

"What would you say if a woman became head of a corporation, Ralphie – would it baffle you?"

The problem was, corporations in general baffled Ralphie because he didn't know anything about them, so he didn't see what the difference would be, one way or the other. But no matter – it seemed to Vera that corporations, lawyers, and professions were signposts to success if women accomplished them. And Ralphie, who had never known what to do with his life, seemed baffled and worried that he would say the wrong thing. And then he would smile and say joyously: "I don't have any idea about them!" Hoping really that this would get him off the hook.

Vera wanted to get straight all of what she no longer believed in, and all of what she believed in. It was important that all of this be settled immediately. One thing she wanted Ralphie to oversee was her lifelong fight with her mother, but as long as Adele was in the room, Vera would speak in a cryptic way, which she had to do for the sake of discretion.

"How is she?"

"Good, good," Ralphie would say.

And while they spoke like this, with Ralphie walking about the room, his hair white and dusty, and his eyes blinking as they always did when he was mulling over something, Adele would sit there, looking in wonder at them both.

Adele did not know what Vera was talking about very often, but how Vera talked, how she thought, made an impression upon her nonetheless.

For example, Adele only had a few things to wear. She had a couple of pairs of corduroys, a few pairs of jeans, some blouses, and the dresses that she had to wear to school. Since she had always been poor she didn't know anything about dressing to look poor. However, it seemed as far as Vera was concerned, the less you considered your clothes or your looks, the better you were. And now Adele was always afraid of dressing too well in front of her. Or wearing make-up, which Vera hated.

But the most particular thing Adele was worried about was that she might like something that Vera did not like, or show that she was foolish by saying something that Vera would not approve of.

For instance, Vera did not approve of *any* of the movies that Ralphie and she went to see, where they ate licorice and drank pop. Ralphie would say: "Well we like um – that's why we go see them – it's fun." And he would say *fun* and look at her, half apologetic about this fun-business.

Ralphie would then brighten up again, and ask her if she still played the piano every day. She used to wake him up in the morning practising Mozart. She had taken piano lessons and studied hard at the convent. She never did anything with friends. Thelma bought her a pair of reachers for her fifteenth birthday and she went to a skating party at the cove, and came home early with frosted fingers, and said someone asked her about her privates. Then she had to invite someone to her high-school prom and didn't want to, and Ralphie, who had never seen Vera

94

go on a date, got a chair ready at five o'clock in the afternoon and sat in the hallway waiting for her boyfriend to arrive. Then Vera came downstairs in her long pink gown with her hair all done up in a thousand knotty little curls, which made her nose seem to be the most prominent part of her. Her father made too much of a fuss over her, walking around her and saying how beautiful she was.

Then she trooped out the door – with her first cousin.

*

When she went to university in 1967, things changed. At first she wrote home, but then after a time the letters stopped. Then they heard a rumour she was dating a black man, and walking about town with him, arm in arm, which made Thelma insomniac. They telephoned her, asked her questions, got into a shouting match, told her to come home. She said she would come home at Thanksgiving, with him.

"You are not bringing anybody like *him* here – like the Belgian Congo or something – and have everyone *saying things*," Thelma said. "Think of your father for one minute. Think of people here in town. And just remember who paid your tuition. If he knew it was a place like that, and everything going on now with these drugs – which make children hate their parents – and getting mixed up with professors, who now that they got a few degrees under their belts have become hippies, well, then – fine, Vera, fine. That's just fine – little girl – that's just fine."

Ralphie listened to one side of the argument and then the other. The world – the outside world – had suddenly crashed in on them.

They got Ralphie to take a day off school and go to

Fredericton to talk with her. Vera was pleased with her father's and mother's reaction, and a new Vera had come to the surface. A Vera who wanted more than anything else to be a Vera, and had wanted her mother and father to react just exactly like they did.

Vera stayed away that Thanksgiving, and on into Easter.

She did not come home and did not write, and the addresses they heard she lived at took on a peculiarly ominous tone.

"My God – what did I do to deserve this?" Thelma would ask when Ralphie came in from school. "She's living in a house on University Avenue for godssake!"

Why this was so bad no one knew, but Thelma felt that it was. Then she felt that Vera was ungrateful and trying to ruin things for them.

The big house suddenly displayed in its physical presence that winter all the problems the family was suffering. The windows were closed by white curtains, the upstairs felt cold when you walked through it. Every night, Ralphie would take his net and hockey stick and go out on the street, riddled and panned with ice, and take slapshots from the driveway with its high snowbanks until Thelma called him in for supper.

Ralphie did not know what to think about all of this. But then he began receiving letters from Vera. Thelma would hand him the letters, with the same look on her face he noticed the night she found out he was dating "the little Walsh kid." Vera had drawn flowers and bees all over the envelopes.

"Look at that," Thelma would say almost hysterically. "Flowers and bees – flowers and bees."

Vera would write these letters using sayings she believed would impress her brother, always with that ironic irreverence towards the older generation – because they had made mistakes she herself had not yet had time to make.

Vera and he had never been close, but now this pretence that they were close, and that Vera could only write to him, overshadowed his life. He was fifteen at that time and wanted to play road hockey and go to school, and liked a girl called Janie Mannie – whom everyone called JayMay – and he always thought of her like you would think of a bluebird.

14

For a while that fall, Joe worked in the woods again. He would get out on the weekends, but during the week he would stay in his camp in the woods. He was cutting for a small mill in Renous. All about him was cut wood, piled haphazardly here or there, the smell of smoke and wet snow on the branches of black trees. He liked using a chainsaw and it didn't bother him so much if he was sore in the morning. However there was one noticeable difference. That is, the way Rita looked at him when he came home on the weekends. She looked upon him now as if he was doing something that he couldn't do. He had seen that look before, as concerned other men, but he had never reflected on it, and it had never bothered him. But now he looked upon this with a new perspective. She would pretend that she didn't look this way, and that she wasn't concerned about him, and she would growl at him for not taking his boots off, or leaving a set of cables on the seat of the truck – but all of this was done differently, as if she was worried about him and his back. He would hang his pants up over the door and lie down beside her, and she would tell him that Adele was acting strange, that Milly tried to paint two children with black paint, or that someone telephoned to ask about the fly rod that he was doing for them – yet all of this also was quite different. When he flinched or was sore she would sometimes look over at him, and then pretend she hadn't noticed it.

On Saturdays, Allain Garret and he would go partridge hunting, and Joe would walk through the woods on small roads, bathed in cold light, as the partridge fanned themselves in the gravelled dirt. At noon they would stop, boil water, and make themselves black tea – strong and thick and smelling of old poplar twigs – but Joe would always find that Rita had packed him something in his lunch that was special. And why this bothered him, as he looked up through the treetops to the blue sky, he did not know. He also felt that Rita had said something to Allain about him. The old man would look over at him, smiling in gratitude and kindness, at whatever Joe said.

During the week he lived in a trailer. The trailer was made of plywood, and its windows were single pane. Sometimes one of the men from the mill would come in and stay a night with them and then leave before breakfast.

Joe did not talk about himself at all. He was so strong he could use his arms instead of his back most of the time anyway. With his chainsaw going all day long, and with limbing and throwing trees out of the way, and working his way along the section he was cutting, he worked from just after dawn until just after dark most of the time.

Because Joe was big, the other men often tried, in good fun, to throw him on his back. Some of the smaller men would give little whoops and jump out of the woods at him, and he would step sideways and push them down. Then some more of their buddies would try it. Joe would be taking a break, tightening his chainsaw chain or putting more lubricant on, and he would hear a noise coming from the woods behind him. He would look about and see no one at all. But then as he turned back to his work, with a ham sandwich stuck in his mouth, he would hear the crack of a white birch twig, and look about again and see the top of a hat sticking up over the snow. He would turn about and smile, and bite down on his sandwich. Then he would see a stick coming out, and a belt tied to it, as they tried to snag his lunch bucket and haul it back into the woods. Just as they thought it was accomplished he would pick up a hunk of maple and drive it at the fellow. "Run the Jesus away from me lunch!" he would yell.

He and a friend of his, Hector Runze, who had become one of the more reckless men Joe had ever known, stayed pretty close together. And sometimes the six others would team up against them in wars of attrition and wits.

Hector, sitting on a stool in his humphrey pants, and looking out over the top of his eyes, would smile. "We'll ambush them – tomorrow morning, even before they go in to cut," he would say. "What I have to do tonight is rig up some sort of tree stand, and get up it – and then I'll have a little surprise for them, mister man."

Then Hector would go about, planting the dynamite in the snow and running a wire, and getting things ordered. It might take him two days to do it.

In fact, with the dynamite business it actually took him a week and a half to set it up properly, and Joe had forgotten completely about it. Until one morning when the rest of the men headed out into the woods, walking along, and as usual planning their offence for the day, there was a *kaboom* to their left, down in the cut, and everyone went scrambling up over the hill through the woods, while Hector sat in the tree laughing, two big Kleenex sticking out of his ears.

What the other men tried to do was separate them from one another and take them on one at a time. And the trailer itself, though small, became sectioned off into war camps. Joe and Hector would look out from behind their clothes they had put up to dry for the night, while the other men had mattresses or boxes shoved up in front of them. Then suddenly a boot would fly across the room, or a pan of some kind, and war would erupt again.

There was a general truce during supper hour or a card game, or when someone was injured, like when Willie, who stood five foot four, tried to swing a stick at Joe and broke his own nose doing it.

And in spite of this, the work went on each and every day.

Nor did Joe tell Dr. Hennessey he was working in the woods, because he knew all hell would break loose. Hennessey had told him he could never work in the woods again, and if he ever found out he was doing it, he would get him fired.

One evening, though, it was Joe's turn to get water down at the brook, and he went along with his aluminum buckets. It was before supper and the woods were still, with the smell of ash and tree trunks rising up out of circular spools of snow, while everything grew darker along the footpath where he walked. It was up a slippery incline, and carrying two buckets filled with water, where he was attacked; he didn't have time to put down his buckets, nor to use them as a weapon. When they grappled him by the legs he couldn't hold his ground, and dropping his buckets, he went backwards, tumbling and sliding toward the brook.

When he stopped sliding he knew he'd hurt his back again. The men tried to lift him to his feet, but he couldn't stand, and they had to rig up a stretcher and carry him back to the trailer. It was the end of their war, but it was also the end of Joe's job. He went home, and spent a week in bed.

*

When he got back on his feet again, Joe would sometimes go to the curling club to watch Rita curl. Vye and Myhrra curled as well. Vye once upon a time had promised Joe a job at the mill where he worked. Joe liked Vye and had always liked people who were friendly to him. Vye always cursed and carried on unless women were present. As soon as a woman was present, Vye would look stone-faced at anyone who cursed.

Now Myhrra and he were inseparable. He was always friendly to Joe and always asked him how the hunting and fishing were going, things which he did not do himself. So every time he saw him Joe would wait in the background until Vye finished doing something. Often Vye would be frowning, but the moment he saw Joe he would brighten up and exclaim something – about things which both he and Myhrra had decided Joe must have an interest in. Or he would ask Joe how he was.

"Good, good," Joe would say, smiling, looking down at the man wearing a big yellow tie, and then he'd start to stutter. Vye would listen to him, with friendly impatience as Joe explained how he was waiting for word from his applications. He never mentioned the mill. Vye would nod, and laugh at some joke Joe made. Then he would look out at the ice.

Joe would stand there, lumbering over him, and smile, nod, not only to Vye, but to others around him when they came in, with a tear in his left boot and his woollen sock sticking out. Then he would clomp outdoors again, walking carefully along in the cold and go down to the rink to watch some intermediate hockey.

Vye, like everyone else, knew about Rita. She was from down river. She had been at first year teacher's college, and had had a boyfriend, but then for some reason ended up marrying Joe. And all of this seemed to him to be exactly the way things would be with her. He knew her family, and how she used to take care of her relatives, cooking for them from the time she was ten.

"Hi, Rita, how are you right now!" he would shout when he saw her on the street the early part of that winter. Rita would have a scarf around her face, tied at the back of her neck in a knot, as the sun shone on the shovelsful of sand covering the ice, hauling two sleds of children along the sidewalk – so that all you saw were heads bobbing and puffs of breath coming.

"I'm fine," she would say. Then she would rush back and pin Doreen's mitts on, or make sure Tammy's hat was straight, or rush back to pick up a toy that one of the kids had dropped, her legs sturdy and tears in her eyes from the wind.

Once Vye had asked Joe about the old mill Allain Garret owned at one time, and if Joe knew who he bought it off, or whatever became of the equipment. But after he asked this question he forgot about asking it, and didn't think Joe would go about the river talking to people to get the information, and then come back one night when he was sitting at the curling club. Nor did Joe know until he did all this, that it would embarrass him. And sometimes when he went there Rita looked embarrassed as well. Rita was embarrassed with Joe at this time because she did not want Joe to embarrass himself. So she was always interrupting him when he spoke.

When people told Joe they would get him a job, Joe never thought that they were just talking – he always assumed that they would.

When Joe saw Vye he would often think of how busy he was, and how important, and he would try not to bother him. And Vye would look busy at just that instant, without even wanting to, perhaps, and later on he would point his finger, and say: "How's everything, Joe?" And Joe would nod and smile.

One night, however, when he thought Joe had left the building, because the outside door had slammed, Vye turned to Myhrra. "Good job – I told you to tell me if you see him coming. I don't need to put up with Joe Walsh."

For a second, Joe smiled because he thought Vye knew he was still there, and was teasing him. But suddenly he realized that no one knew he was there. He was alone in the hallway. A storm was coming, there was a sound of a plough on the street, and all the buildings looked secretive and warm all of a sudden. Then he left the building and walked slowly off into the dark.

Rita said she wanted Joe to curl with her, and he said he would. Everything was fine yet when he went out onto the ice he felt uncomfortable. He found it hard to keep down in the hack for any length of time. Vye was his instructor, and he showed him how to hold a broom and how to differentiate between the turns. But for some reason, Joe felt he could not fit in with them.

Joe stood there watching, as Rita showed what she had learned. Then he picked up two stones and started to carry them about with him, lifting them over his shoulder, as if to make fun not only of his strength but of his general igno-rance of the game. He had dug out an old red sweater from his closet, which he thought Rita would want him to wear. But when he looked at her, he realized he must have worn the wrong one, and when he threw a stone it broke the ice, wobbled, and came to a sudden halt. Then they tried a make-up game and Joe got more and more embarrassed.

And suddenly it was settled, at forty-three everything was the way it should be, and there was nothing that shouldn't be the way it was. And he felt that he had let her down in everything and this was just one more thing he would let her down with – because he felt he couldn't and didn't want to curl. He couldn't curl because he felt Rita didn't want him to. And yet if he told anyone, this is what he sensed, and it was the real reason he didn't curl, not only wouldn't they agree with him but they wouldn't find any evidence that would support how he felt.

What made him feel guilty was the fact that Rita had ordered him curling shoes.

"You don't understand," she had said, "you have to curl."

And yet still he felt that some part of her didn't want him to. But worse was that Rita had an entertainment allow-ance, and she had ordered his shoes from this, and as always this simple act made him sorry for her – as if all her money and hopes, and envelopes in the kitchen drawer over the years, had come to nothing.

"What do you mean I have to curl? I don't have to curl at all if I goddamn don't want to, and no one can make me. Besides, all the teams are made up – and you have a team to play on, so go out and have a good time."

Walking through the woods one night he thought of this. It was fine if she curled. Actually she should curl. It would be good if she did curl, and that settled it.

Joe also wanted Adele's opinion on this. But Adele said

105

nothing. She just got angry at him for mixing her up when she was trying to do her new math – and she told him so. And quick as always to defend her anger, she said:

"All's I know if you don't smarten up and take some stock of yourself we'll all be living alone before New Year's, every last one of us – and I don't mind – but Milly can't stand it – her whole potential is being missed – and what if you have another kid."

"I don't think . . ." Joe began.

"But that's the problem with you, Joe – you don't think very well at all, it's as if your brain had turned to plant food or something as bad as that, and you have to take care of Mom – you shouldn't let her go out alone because I know *people* and *you* don't. I know a heck of a lot more than you think. I had ulcers so I should know. She curls with those lads and I don't like them. And they have *real* jobs and stuff like that there – how can you let her curl with them!" she said, enraged, and standing up with one shoe on and one shoe off. "You never think – you never do, and ruin my concentration!" she yelled. And then she went about banging her shoe against the bedroom wall, and throwing cushions about and talking about the past, where everything was wrong, and everything was wrong because it disagreed with her.

One night Joe was sitting alongside Rita in the living room. She knew his leg was bothering him, the way he was holding it. Then he got up and paced back and forth.

"How's yer back?"

"Not too bad," he said. "Pretty good – it's okay."

He looked out the window as he said this, as if this glance confirmed everything he had just said – when to Rita it proved just the opposite.

He turned about and looked at her.

"I'm sorry I can't curl," he said. "But I never know when I can get down in the hack." He smiled.

"Goddamn back on you," Rita said. They didn't look at each other as they spoke.

Joe had been to a number of doctors but now he refused to go to any. He was very stubborn now about doctors. A look of mistrust came into his eyes when someone mentioned a new back cure they had read of in a magazine. Or a new mattress. Rita was always mentioning new mattresses – and one could tell how aggravated he got over this talk. It was as if a person was discussing with him a subject where from the very moment they began the discussion they missed the entire crux of the problem – which he alone knew – and he had to listen further to theories on treatments that were like the other treatments.

Joe had been to doctors and to therapy, and there was an operation he could have. Dr. Hennessey suggested he go to St. John and have it when he decided to.

Rita asked him if he wanted her to rub his back.

"No no," Joe said, "that's Adele's job."

"I can do it," Rita said.

"No no no," Joe said.

And then, resting his hands against the wall, he slid down carefully, smiling at the pain.

"If you don't get to the outpatients tomorrow, I'll kill you," Rita said.

Joe went to the outpatients the next day. He sat in the waiting room for two hours with his cap in his hand, looking at people coming and going. Finally he got in to see Dr.

Savard. The doctor got him to take off his shirt. He looked at his arms. Then he got him to move his leg back and forth.

"Have you been into therapy?" Savard asked, in the same tone Joe had heard a dozen times before. There was always a hint that it was his fault all of this had happened.

Savard's small hands felt Joe's back and got him to loosen his pants. Joe sniffed and looked about. He hated the hospital. He hated to look at the other people there – for the simple reason he felt he was intruding upon them. For instance when he'd passed by the x-ray room, he happened to see a woman in a bra folding her shirt carefully over a chair. At any other time he might have thought he was fortunate. But at this moment he felt sad. The bra was very clean and white, as if she was attempting to wear the proper things, and do things diligently now that she was here – just like everyone else in the world.

Joe nodded as they spoke. The room was hot. The little nurse with a watch inverted on her left breast, and her hands dry and warm, took his blood pressure, and leaned against him as he sat on the gurney. He could feel the inside of her left leg.

The doctor asked him if he was on painkillers.

"The back is a hard machine," Joe said, smiling in embarrassment. "Lots a days she don't bother me none at all."

Savard nodded in agreement. Then he wrote Joe a prescription and Joe went home.

He put the prescription in the pocket of his coat and forgot about it.

15

One night a short time later, Joe told Rita he'd meet her at the club. But he didn't get out of the house until late. He kept trying to find his belt, which he was sure had been on his pants earlier that day. He and Milly searched the house for it. Every once in a while Adele would stop writing her history essay – she had suddenly become much more conscientious about work – and would lift up a cushion and look under it, or feel with two fingers down the back of the lazyboy chair.

Then Joe had to break up a fight because Milly called Adele fat. Adele said she was not fat, and hit her across the head. Then Ralphie came in and she got cross at him for not meeting her that morning and she roared at him that he had broken their pact. Then Joe decided to go.

The lane was dark, yet the sky shone orange against the tops of the trees. He started the truck and it stalled, and he had to get out and open the hood and put a screwdriver into the starter. Adele watched him from the window, with a forlorn look on her face as if she realized at that moment that no matter how well her father could fix things, he never had the money to do things the way they should be done.

He waved to her and Milly. Their house was yellow and green and its windows were larger than need be. But Joe never had the money to finish it exactly the way he wanted to, although he had done a fairly good job inside the house.

When he was drinking he would give away what he had, only to end up borrowing it back from the person he had loaned it to, sometimes having to pay a price. He had given away ideas and information about his various businesses that the competition used to put him out of business – and he could never understand it. When he was drinking he had given away trade secrets that seemed to have done him in – and yet nothing could be said about it. He also would give away money to people who had more money than he did in their pockets. Rita would stand over him, hitting him on his big wide head, with anything she could find, a sneaker, a boot, a pan, asking him where the money was:

"I don't know," Joe would say, puzzled. "I have no idea – what, don't you have it?"

At times she would beat him until she cut his head open and the blood flowed down over his face. But he would only shrug and not know what to say. So as she beat him he would take a stubborn turn and refuse to answer her.

Tonight because he didn't have any money on him, Adele had given him five dollars. She had run downstairs and handed it to him as if, since he was going up to the curling club she didn't want him to embarrass her mother. Or perhaps she didn't want him to embarrass himself. Whatever the reason, it was the first time she had given him any money – or anything else.

Adele, since she could count change, had been so stingy

she squeaked. She was even mean to herself. For years she had hoarded away her Hallowe'en candy until it rotted in its pillowcase and they had to fight with her even then to throw it out.

One night a month Adele bought a pizza from money she had saved. She might give Milly a sliver or a piece of hamburger at the bottom of the box – and Milly could have whatever dropped on the floor.

Once, when Joe was temporarily blinded by a flash when he had his welding job, he lay on the couch with tea bags on his eyes. The house smelled of tea bags, and scribblers from school, and torn covers of schoolbooks. Outside, the river was yellow and the window rattled.

When Adele came home from school and saw him lying on the couch, she decided at that instant that she needed to make a cup of tea. Except the only two tea bags in the house were on Joe's eyes.

"I need those bags," she said.

"Well," Joe said, "you can't have them. As you see, I need them and they are on me eyes."

"For your information, Joe, which ya are so stupid about half the time," Adele screamed, "I'm having my period. I think for sure ya'd not know that Mom has said I'm to have tea because it stabilizes my system, up and down, so there you go."

With that, Joe lifted a tea bag up and looked at her and she snatched it off of his eye and ran into the kitchen.

No one else knew that Adele was not his daughter but he and Rita. Joe had been in the woods that summer. Rita was working for the recreation council. She became pregnant before Joe ever touched her. The boy who was responsible went to Windsor without knowing of it. After this, Rita accepted the idea that she and Joe get married. That is, after he came out of the woods she began to notice him more. He loved everything about her. He loved the way she moved, the way she worked, the way she smiled. When he asked her to marry him – he had been thinking of asking her for over a year – he stuttered and flushed. She was working out in her yard. She was bent over trying to clear some bushes about this old telephone post. And Joe, before he knew what he was doing, lifted the telephone post out of the ground and held it up while she clipped. Then he set it down gently and smiled. When he looked at her she was crying, and he did not know why. Finally just before they were to be married she told him. Rita was worried, and couldn't sleep or eat, and kept going out of her way to try and please him. And because of this he spent more and more time alone in the tavern. He always felt that he didn't deserve her, and therefore some day she would go away.

Her hair in a ponytail and her pink maternity top, and even the way she carried the baby, which made her gain a lot of weight, bothered Joe at this time. When Adele was born Joe left the house for a month, and came back later, knocking on the door with his hat in his back pocket.

Adele very early tried to learn how to get him to like her and was always waiting up for him. And each time he came home (he was driving truck at this time) she would run to him. For five or six years he felt uncomfortable with her. And then one day, when he woke up after being drunk, he saw her. She was grumbling to herself, going about with a broom and a dustpan. She had her mother's apron on and was walking around with a ribbon in her hair, grumbling

and complaining about something. From that day forward
his feeling changed toward her but it was not until another
four years had passed that he began to love her as he did
now.

When he got to the club the game was over and Rita was at
the door. She was all alone glancing back over her
shoulder. When he spoke she looked at him and smiled
timidly, and he felt suddenly that she was disappointed he
had come. And just then her friends came around the
corner. Joe smelled alcohol and he realized that they were
going out the door together and that he had intruded.

For some reason Rita looked like Milly at that moment,
looking up at him and holding her broom and smiling.
Then he saw Gloria Basterashe. For some reason she disliked him and Joe had always felt uncomfortable because
of the way she looked at him. He never knew what to say to
her and often stuttered when he spoke to her. And he felt
that Gloria did not like him, and there was nothing he
could do. And when he looked at Gloria now the same
feeling that he had done something wrong filled him.
Then he nodded and smiled.

When Myhrra saw Joe come into the curling club she
started to speak in an animated and unnatural way, as if
everything they had been talking about was some special
thing that he, a mere sober person, would not understand.
This was almost always the case with those who did not
drink a lot. Myhrra wore eye shadow that sparkled over her
eyes tonight, and purple lipstick that matched her purple
gloves, and yet this made her not younger looking but

older. She talked as if she had organized everything, and they were all going somewhere special together.

"Oh, Joe – you're too late, your wife has been captured. We're a real drunken crew, I'm afraid." Then she looked away.

Vye was standing in the background with a sober expression. He said they were all off to have a drink, and just to prove he had drunk more than he had, he grabbed Gloria and kissed her. Joe smiled, and looked over at Myhrra, who suddenly looked glum. Rita said nothing, she only clung to her wallet, which was in her left hand.

Rita wanted to go. And if she wanted to go, Joe wanted her to, only he couldn't go with her. Everyone was happy, everyone was drinking, and therefore they should go. But he couldn't go with them.

"I have the deciding vote on this," Vye said. "And I say Rita comes with us."

"And I'm head of the campaign," Myhrra said, looking about and nodding.

Rita smiled and looked at Joe.

"I'll pay, honest I will," Myhrra said for some reason.

"Did you win?" Joe asked looking at them, as if this was what he was supposed to say, and yet feeling he was being forced into saying that.

"Yes, Joe, we won, we won. Now, are you coming?" Gloria asked, somehow put out by the innocent question.

"Come on – I bet Rita wants you to go," Vye said.

Joe looked at Vye, his eyes half closed, but he said nothing for a moment. It didn't matter to him, yet every one of them believed it did.

"Not tonight," he said.

"Well, good," Gloria said. "You won't mind if she comes with us, will you? I promise to take good care of her."

"She doesn't have to ask my permission," Joe said, stuttering and trying not to look at Gloria at all.

"It's a new age," Myhrra said. "Everyone can have fun!" Then she took a curt step up, beside Vye.

Joe cocked his head a little and still didn't look Rita's way. He just smiled.

He felt that something awful was happening that had nothing to do with the conversation, or Rita going, it had nothing to do with that. It had much more to do with whether or not Joe proved to them that he was the person they already assumed he was. And this was always, when it came down to it, what a person such as Joe had to prove, or disprove.

He looked about, nodded to no one in particular, and left.

Rita followed Joe outside. Snow was coming down gently, and Vye carried his gloves in his hand and walked out into the soft dark snow behind them, singing a new song. Joe was angry, and when he put the hood of the truck up to start it with a screwdriver, he tore one side of the hood off.

"What is it?" Rita asked, looking worried.

"Nothing," he said.

And, angrier still, he wrenched the hood with his arms and tried to lift it completely off.

"Won't the truck start?" Rita said.

"Yes, the truck will start," he said. He took some snuff and put it into his mouth, and then spit.

"Well, Rita can come home with us," Vye said, standing behind him.

"Go on – with them," Joe whispered. "Go on, go with them. I can fix the sonofabitch."

"I'll stay here," she said, holding the handle of her new curling broom. And Joe felt that he wasn't understood and had nothing more to say. And besides this, he had upset Rita for no reason.

Rita got into the truck and sat there with a scarf tied under her chin, and looked out the window at him.

It wasn't her fault if he did not feel comfortable doing the things she wanted to do. He always felt uncomfortable with people she knew because he could never think of anything to say to them. And Rita was afraid he was going to say something or do something that would embarrass her. Yet he knew people didn't care why someone didn't drink when they themselves were having a good time. The only thing was, that in everyone who presumed because of drink that they had suddenly become authentic, Joe saw himself.

The next morning when he woke up he decided to go hunting. They had just had a snowfall and there was a week left in the season. It did not really matter if he went alone or brought Milly with him. The only thing that mattered to him at this moment was to get out of the house. He went into the old part of the basement where he kept his fishing rods and reels, his trophies and guns. The window above him was green, and snow had piled up over it. He packed his knapsack with compass and rope, with his skinning knife and a small whetstone. Everything he did at this moment, however, seemed deliberate – as if it wasn't really him packing up to go.

Rita did not have the kids that morning and decided to go to the new mall. After he started the truck for her and shoved the screwdriver into her back pocket, Joe went back into the house and sat at the table, rolled a cigarette, and suddenly picked up an ashtray and threw it against the wall.

*

Sometimes when Joe took Milly with him to the woods, they'd sleep under a lean-to. He'd make it with tarp between two trees, brace it with rope or wire, and light a fire out front, spread the coals at the entrance, place boughs in the back, make him and Milly a bed, and hunker in for the night. He would stare up at the stars, and smell smoke, and listen to Milly's stories. He'd do this whenever they were too far from camp to make it back. He did this often when he was alone, just to do it.

Tonight Joe was making their lean-to near the brook about a mile and a half from his camp, while Milly sat on a tree that had fallen over and told him about her favourite TV shows, "Scoobie Doo," and "Star Trek."

"So then what happened?" Joe asked.

"The monssir got him by the throat."

"By whose throat?"

"Oh – Captain Kirk."

"And then what?"

"A faser," Milly said, yawning. "Got him with a faser."

Joe could never follow what his daughter was saying.

After the lean-to was set up Joe brought her some soup which he had made in a pan over the coals. Because the cup was too hot for her, Joe held it for her while she drank. The evening was just getting dark. Joe looked cautiously about.

"You know we might see a moose tonight, Milly."

The little girl nodded as if she knew this. She had been with Joe last year when they hauled a bull out of the woods, on the back of a truck. When they got home, Milly stepped out of the truck, covered in blood, and began spitting. Rita had to take her inside and scrub her for almost an hour while she screeched and roared. But Joe did not hunt moose this year. It was one more thing that since he was sober he decided not to do.

Joe sat down beside her and drank from his own cup of soup. As the evening got darker, everything seemed further away. There was a boulder a ways off that seemed to disappear, and the white-pebbled brook beneath them took on a stranger and more insistent bellow.

They sat together on the log with Milly's feet hanging down but not touching the ground, and Joe rolling himself a cigarette. There was a wind, and it was cold on his ears. The gloom made the old spruces and stumps take on the shapes of animals and people. It settled down over the earth. The branches quivered in the dark area. A strange flower that had not yet died stuck up out of a torn piece of earth, and there was a shiver in the smell of dusk. Although only twenty miles from town they could have been a thousand miles.

"Are you cold, darlin?" he said after a time, lost in his thoughts.

"No," Milly said.

"Well, I'm going to make some hot chocolate – so you go over to the lean-to and get down in the sleeping bag, and I'll go to the brook."

After the hot chocolate Milly lay down and began to rock back and forth and Joe lit the Coleman lantern and checked his rifle.

A buck had made two scrapes just north of where they had built the lean-to. There was a doe travelling with a fawn, and another doe that was travelling alone in this heavy wooded area of mixed stands and gravel slopes and furious little brooks.

As Milly slept, Joe oiled and cleaned the barrel of his rifle, outside away from the shelter, and made mental notes to himself on how he would travel the next day. He did not like hunting with Milly, but now that she was here, in her little red coat and hat, walking about as if she alone knew all about the woods, he would take her with him. To do this he began to rig the basket he had with him so she could rest on his back as he walked.

Then as he tightened the last strap on the basket and slipped into it, to see if it was comfortable riding on his shoulders, he thought of the truck and the hood and Vye in his fur hat outside the curling club, and someone saying: "She can come with us."

And, bothered by this, he flinched his strong shoulders, threw the basket off to the side and, putting his hands in his pockets, made a stabbing motion in the dirt with his foot.

16

Rita went out that night with Myhrra and didn't get home until three in the morning. When she got into the house, and Myhrra honked her horn as she drove away, Adele was sitting on the stairs with a bowl of ice cream, listening to the wind and, with her housecoat and knitted slippers on, looking like she was dressed in a tea cozy.

"I suppose Dad and Milly are going to freeze their holes out tonight," Adele said, licking the back of the spoon. Rita put down her black purse, and rummaged in the drawer for a package of cigarettes.

"Do you have a cigarette, Delly – I'm out."

"How do you know if I smoke or not?" Adele asked. Then from under her armpit she hauled a package of Cameos.

"They'll be alright," Rita said. "Joe could go into the woods with a blanket and a bag of flour and last all winter."

"Well, it seems to me that some people don't care if their wonderful little Milly lies tits up in the woods."

"You've been in the woods with Joe and you got out alright."

"That's because I do the worrying in this goddamn family," Adele said, crying suddenly, and she set her bowl on the step and walked upstairs, with the padded bottom of her slippers pouncing on the floor. Just then a huge gale came up, a tree made a loud crack, and her little slippers padded silently away. When she got to the bathroom she suddenly felt sick and threw up, waving her hands frantically to keep Rita away from her.

"And I want to tell you about some of the people – some of them are sleazy, sleazy people, Mom – and you are going out booten around with that Gloria Basterache."

Rita came to the top of the stairs, and with her hand on the banister she spoke, and Adele put her hands over her ears.

"I don't care about her," Rita said. "She's Myhrra's friend." Rita's hand on the banister looked white in the light of the hall. Joe's red sweater lay over a chair in the hallway. "I don't have a lot in common with Gloria Basterache."

"You do so!" Adele screeched. "You and Gloria Basterache."

"I don't care about her," Rita said. "Don't get me angry."

"Well, I don't like her – and who I don't like is no good – so you just remember that," Adele screeched. "I worry all night and then I get sick to my stomach and it's the same all over again. As long as you go work for people they will make a hump of fun about you. And they don't like Joe and make fun of his stuttering attacks, and I heard that Gloria was just the one to make some fun of his stutter. How could you go out with anyone who makes fun of his stutter!" She said suddenly breaking into tears again. "And Myhrra is just led along by the nose as always. She's been hanging about a little too much with all those useless people!" Then her door slammed. "And that is my final word!"

Everything that had happened bothered Rita as well. Joe

standing at the curling club door, his huge frame against the outside light, the hood of the truck, and Gloria looking up at him, and then over at Rita.

They all said they were glad he wasn't drinking. They all hoped he would not drink again. But she felt they wanted Joe to drink and she could not deny this. And sometimes she herself hoped he would drink. She also knew that people who didn't even know her sympathized with her because of him, but she knew also that it was a sympathy that had been manufactured by Myhrra and others – it was forced and had nothing to do with Joe, whom they did not know or care for. And sometimes Vye would give her arm a squeeze, and nod to her in a patronizing way.

The first time Joe quit drinking it surprised her. This was some years before. Rita celebrated by getting drunk and falling backwards off the steps and twisting her ankle. Joe went outside and picked her up by the belt and carried her back into the house while she sang at the top of her lungs.

Unfortunately, a week later, her two brothers arrived from Lethbridge, Alberta, and they wanted Joe to show them everything and take them everywhere, and be the same as they were.

Joe acted as if he was shy of them, because he didn't know how to act with them when he was sober. They complained about everything here, because everything here, back east, was evidently not as wonderful as where they were now from. And Joe listened to this, and also to the complaining that things they had expected to be the same were now, somehow, different. And, if they could not make Joe drink (which they insisted they didn't want to do), they would ignore him.

Because her brothers were back, and because everything was exciting, Rita forgot about Joe at that time. And one day she came into the upstairs hallway and saw him sitting on the old chair in the corner sweating, though it was not hot, with his hands on his knees, and his duffel bag packed as if he was going to go somewhere. He looked up at her and smiled, in a worried way, and said:

"If I drink now – I'm a real goner."

"Don't worry," she said, in an easy way, "you won't drink – you've gotten it licked!"

That night her brothers wanted to take them out to the new tavern, and busied themselves getting ready, while Joe stood in the kitchen with his hat (a cowboy hat they had brought him) in his hand, with the same worried look on his face. The house smelled of shaving lotion in the early fall air, and there was the scent of cigarettes and beer. The calendar in the kitchen was dated a month behind, and there was a scent of aluminum and tin from outside. The water was grey, and yet huge white clouds with pink bellies floated above. Therefore, the air, the scent of cigarettes and the boys singing, all gave Joe the feeling that it would be good to have a drink – to laugh and talk with a bottle and to forget your troubles.

Joe sat in the tavern with them drinking tomato juice, and Rita found herself discussing old times with her brothers – and all of this, as innocent as it was, was an indication to Joe that he had become an outsider. Then her brothers asked her about her old boyfriend, the one she'd gone with the summer Joe was working in the woods. The brothers did not think that this would be a sensitive subject to Joe. Rita answered bluntly that she had not seen him in years and Joe said nothing. But for the first time because he was not drinking he was not the same.

Her brothers deployed themselves on the couches, and slept on the floors, and every night Joe came home from work and found them already into the booze, and waiting to tell him of some innocent incident that had happened that day. Every night Joe remained an outsider to the one thing he had in common with other men, a capacity and willingness to drink.

And through all of this Joe saw one thing – which he kept in his heart. He saw that her brothers, whom she pampered and protected, acted with no idea of the consequences, and therefore in them he could only see himself.

So one night at the end of two weeks Joe found himself listening to the same stories coming from different bottles. And without even thinking he was going to drink, and drink being the furthest thing from his mind, he could not stop pouring a bottle of wine into himself.

Then Rita, angry with him over this, shouted at him, and he pushed her away with one hand, and she fell on her rump. As soon as they saw Joe drinking, the brothers became sorry for Rita, and told Joe to settle down. And Joe laughed and picked one up by the belt buckle with his teeth and shook him. Then Adele flew into the fray, and hit him on the head with a broom, shouting: "Let go of Uncle Derwood."

And Rita stood and jumped him from behind. Then the other brother, Clement, hit him while they were all swinging him about. Then he shook his shoulders and Rita went flying, and Adele kept following him about, hitting him every step he took, and finally he turned about and grabbed her by her left ear and twisted it.

"Don't ya be twistin little Delly's ear!" Derwood said.

"Don't you touch my ear, you bully," Adele screeched.

Rita came back up flying with both fists then and managed to hit Joe twice in the mouth. Then Derwood and Clement said they would call the cops, and they went to pick up the telephone. But as soon as they did, Adele came to life and tore it out of Clement's hands.

"You're not getting the fucking cops here!" Adele shouted. She banged the receiver down and went at Joe again, fell to her knees, and bit his thigh.

*

The next morning they were all sleeping in different parts of the house. And they woke to rain pouring down over the oil barrel and the sky dark and the September grass wet and cold. Joe was the first up, and he took a bottle of shaving lotion and mixed it with some beer, and sat at the table, shaking. Then Adele got up and dressed to go out. She came downstairs with a huge bandage on her ear that looked like a doughboy was stuck over it. "Well, someone has to go out and get something to eat to keep this family from starving right to death," she said to him.

"Yer not going to wear that goddamn doughboy-looking thing out, are you, darlin?" he said shivering and stuttering.

"I wear what I have to to keep my ear from bleeding right to death. – it's just like the same when I was in Brownies and you come home drunk and mauled all my cookies," Adele said, and she left the house.

When Rita's brothers got up, Joe looked at them and smiled weakly. They both mooched about for a drink and Joe called a taxi to bring up a pint. Then they reprimanded him while he sat there, and painstakingly went over the reasons why he should quit.

Then they boarded the train that night, shaking their heads because he was asking them to stay just one more day, and had followed them to the train.

17

The same fascination with herself that had caused Myhrra to get married, was the same that caused her to get divorced. That is, she saw the doorknob turn and she decided to get married; she was sure Mike would come back to her and she got divorced. They fought over everything, even the coat hangers in the front hall. But this was not done for the reason it seemed to be done, but for the exact opposite reason. The more she took coat hangers, the more Mike kicked her in the bum; the more she scratched his Legion dart trophies, and buried them where he'd never find them again, the more she actually did not want to get divorced at all. They fought. They hauled Byron by the arms, standing out on the street while people looked on, and Byron screeched that they were hauling his limbs off. The more they fought, the more it seemed that they wanted nothing to do with each other. And yet they needed each other as much for the divorce as they did for the marriage.

Now Byron was bringing his friends home and saying he hated her in front of them. He walked about with a dark expression on his face. Though he was only young he scared her and she would always give in to him. He would always make a comment at her expense to make his friends laugh. Then they would go into the bedroom together. He would say: "Hi Mom, how's tits?" Or something like that.

She worried that those friends measured him by how many rude comments he could make to his mother, who was loving to him and had never done him anything wrong.

Myhrra was seeing the priest now as often as possible. With this new crisis in her life, with this feeling of being alone, she needed a priest to talk to. Father Garret, Allain's brother's youngest, a tall, unnaturally thin man, was the priest who counselled her at this time. Using a measure of his sociology classes from university, and his own desire to be looked upon as understanding, along with his abundant dislike of the type of men on the river, especially men like his uncle and Joe Walsh, he gave Myhrra a sympathetic ear. After each visit, Myhrra had the feeling of being pure and good – simply because she had talked to the priest, who of course believed in the "new" church – which she considered much more open. Myhrra liked the fact that people saw her coming and going from the priesthouse or talking to "Father" in the yard.

But still, Mike was remarrying and no one could change that. The priest finally told her this one night when she went to see him.

Everything Father Garret said after that remark took on a different meaning. Instead of liking her, he did not. Instead of being sympathetic, he was jealous of her. Instead of being sensitive, he was filled with that terrible piety. Suddenly she remembered him sitting on a bait box as a boy, out on the wharf. She remembered she was seventeen at the time, and they were playing "Rock around the Clock" and "Whole Lotta Shakin' Goin' On." He had just come from church with his mother, and his feet were covered in dust, and they were gossiping while the sun hit his eyes. Men walked about him, working, their clothes dirty and their faces strong in the wind. He looked over at Myhrra. He was a tall gangly boy. There was some hay on his left shoe.

All of this she saw again in a second, as she stood in his office off the main hallway, and she now felt that they had lied to each other right from the start. That is, she had over-emphasized all of her problems, and he had tried to show a sympathy which he could not really give.

Myhrra left the priesthouse. She walked out into the cold. She lit a cigarette and then another. She smelled burnt paper and railway ties, and she remembered all of the years she was going to go away on one of those trains. Suddenly she cried, and for some reason began to curse Rita.

"Best friend," she said. "Best friend – what friend do I have?" And at this moment she ran toward home in the wind.

Myhrra got Byron ready to go to the wedding. She got him a new white shirt, and found his suit was so small for him he wouldn't be able to wear it. And though she had made comments about Mike and how he was supposed to give her money for child support, it was she herself who went downtown and paid for Byron's new suit. Then she had to get him new shoes.

She wanted Byron to look his best. The night before the wedding, Myhrra had all his clothes laid out. She had taken his new shoes out of the box, and put them at the foot of the bed, and had laid his pants over the chair.

It was a clear night. The air smelled flat and cold. In the trailer, there were little drafts the source of which she hadn't been able to find, no matter how often she'd gone about touching the walls.

*

The next morning when Byron got up he said his egg wasn't cooked right. A little of the yolk was running and he wouldn't eat it. This idea of being pampered whenever he had to do something gave Byron the edge on his mother.

"I don't feel like eating the egg," he said.

"Well, you have to eat it."

"Well, I'm not going to eat it."

Myhrra, who was drinking a coffee, and looking out at the cold, flat, and somehow at that moment spiteful-looking field, told him that he'd better eat it. The smell of the egg, the flat sky, the barren field – all of this depressed her.

He upset the egg and stomped out of the room.

Myhrra didn't bother with him. She got ready and went out to the car and started it.

But when she came back in Byron had his old clothes on and was feeding his guppies.

"I have to drive you up to the church, Byron – you have to be there in a half-hour."

"Not going."

"You are so going."

"Not."

"Are so – you're an usher for christsake."

Myhrra, who hadn't wanted the wedding to happen, and

129

hadn't wanted Byron to go to it, now found herself struggling to get him ready.

Finally she told him he wasn't going to the wedding – and once she told him he wasn't going, he got ready, and ran out the door towards the car, while she followed him with his cuff links and a brush in her right hand, taking swipes at his hair.

When they got into the car Byron held his arms up for her to put the cuff links on, and as she doubled his cuffs and yanked his sleeves down he looked at her.

"You haven't fixed my hair – you just made it all messed up," Byron said to her.

How could he say what he did to her, she who loved him more than anyone else – who had given birth to him?

18

Vera and Nevin had managed to buy a farm using their own savings and a loan from Thelma. Though very stern and practical, Thelma had another common trait – she could not stand not to be a part of her daughter's life, and tried to help her when she could.

One day in December Vera took a walk over her land. It was cold, and snow blew against her face. The trees were white and naked, and the grass seemed to be fierce and cold. Little paths ran off the sides to walls of bleak alders, and above her she could hear the highway as she walked.

Vera came in to visit the doctor, with that assertive step she believed was very new for women. This was the step that had characterized her since her university days, and seemed to make her lankiness more noticeable. She took giant boot steps across the room.

She began to talk about her house down on the shore and how it should have been kept up, but the family who lived there before weren't the type to keep it up. She was unaware that the doctor, as well as everyone on the road, knew and liked this family – she was only sure that with her there, things would finally get done.

Vera was one of those people who is normally infuriating because every new opinion is suddenly hers – and hers alone – and in another year or so she will move on to something else. The very things that in 1968 she argued for, were now vehemently argued against.

After she opened her coat – Vera also had to show that she "dressed for the climate," not like those "other women" who dressed insubstantially – she got the doctor to feel her coat, and then reach down and feel her furry boots.

Then Vera began to complain about Christmas and how it seemed to her to be ridiculously commercial. Whenever she said anything she smiled and then frowned so quickly the person she was talking to was never sure if they'd seen a smile or not.

Finally Dr. Hennessey said – in that polite way he had which made you sure he disliked someone – that he thought Christmases were good, and that he himself was a walking Santa Claus. Vera simply smiled, and frowned once more, and looked about his kitchen. He had a clothesline strung above the sink, and was drying a number of pairs of woollen socks. The radio played, half-static country and western music, and an old tin of sardines lay open upon the table.

"I just get more and more Christmasy every year," the old doctor said, and obviously at that moment, as he stared at Vera, he believed it and would continue to believe it until Vera left his house. The doctor would usually do this when he felt that someone believed they knew who he was or what he was about. Since Vera believed that she alone (or to the doctor it suddenly seemed this way) had found out about Christmas he would not give her the satisfaction of agreeing with her. The doctor knew no moderation in anything and already had decided that he did not like the way she lived or the way she thought.

He'd had to go to town one day last week with his sister-in-law Clare, and while he was there he went in to see Ralphie. Nevin had been there, walking about. The doctor tripped in the doorway, and his hat had come partially off, and he felt that Nevin thought he was quite a foolish old man – and the feeling that Nevin would think this infuriated him.

*

This was the case more and more with the doctor, as he became more and more unwilling to agree with anyone. With his short grey hair and thick shoulders, with his chest bones jutting out, he was strangely imposing. In one way he looked rather pompous and careful, but in another, with his large hands, his penetrating gaze, he always struck people as being formidable and angry.

He generally disliked cruelty of any sort. For example he secretly disliked horse-hauling. He had never gotten used to it. Yet if a person he did not respect thought horse-hauling was cruel, he would be all for horse-hauling. If a person complained that a horse was hyped up on tea, then so much the better – the horse should be hyped up on tea – what was tea for if not to hype up horses. If a person said he wanted to quit drinking because he had a vision of the Virgin Mary – the doctor would say that if he had a vision of the Virgin when he was drinking he would bloody well be a fool to stop.

Vera smiled as she spoke, and with her big calm eyes, looked at him, as if she knew he would not be able to believe all of the brand new things she was now doing. Though she was not consciously trying to impress him with all these new things, she could not help mentioning every detail of how her life had changed. Every time she said anything the doctor nodded, or cleared his throat.

Then, after finishing her apple cider, she put the glass down, stood abruptly and, still smiling, said that she had to go. And this too seemed to explain everything she now was. The doctor gave a start, because he knew that Clare would be waking from her nap and would want to see her. Clare was Vera's godmother. She had taught her to play the piano, and she loved Vera more than she loved anyone else. But since Vera had explained that she was now in a hurry to get home and start supper, the doctor would not ask her to stay.

He hasn't changed, Vera said to herself once outside. *He hasn't changed at all*. The smell of the road, and the pinkish light shining from Madgill's garage made her suddenly feel happy and elated. Everything was more solid at twilight. Up a side road some children played. She did not realize that she was feeling the greatness of the river that she was once again upon. The very trees and houses made her feel this way.

With her hands in her pockets she took some assertive steps towards the lower fields, her hair blowing behind her and her large ears bare.

The barn was dark at the end of the field, and Vera often went out there after dark to check on the horses. She had bought an old horse and she would not admit she had made a bad deal. Sometimes Ralphie would come down to help her pile wood in the cellar, and hear the horse coughing in the stall. There was some dry hay, so the horse was always coughing, and the smell of frozen dung. Far across the bay on a clear day you could see the tip of one of the nearest islands. Above them, but still far away, there was the church – one of the oldest Catholic churches in the province where Aunt Clare went to church every evening at seven o'clock. Ralphie had to put the eight-foot wood on a sawhorse and cut it. Then he had to split it on a splitter. It was then loaded into a wheelbarrow that was made out of slats of rough pine, not unlike a trough. Vera pushed this wheelbarrow to the window, and with leather mitts on her hands and her arms scratched, she unloaded the wood into the cellar. Even though it was cold, they were sweating. The sun was pale, and there was the look of milk in the woods. The stream that ran down to the small pond was frozen, and the wood road was hard with snowy mud and sloughs. Vera teetered and stumbled under her burden, her thin legs staggering and her mouth clamped shut.

"Well, what do you think of Nevin?" Vera said one day when Ralphie was wiring her bathroom. She was wearing a scarf about her head, and her granny glasses sloped down on her nose. She had worked for five hours straight, without a rest, to try and insulate the inside of the house. Her shirt was torn open and he could see one of her breasts, with a mole on its side. Some white winter light came in on those glasses and made them reflective. She wore an old orange shirt that had once belonged to Ralphie. She had a pair of black slacks on, which hung off her skinny hips and made her bum look small as she walked about, and, noticing this, Ralphie felt sad and looked puzzled.

"He knows what I've gone through, and he would never let me down. . . ."

And drawing on the false notion, since the letters of 1967, that she and Ralphie were very close – and in fact she had taken Ralphie and Adele under her wing – she smiled.

"He's alright," Ralphie said, blushing. Ralphie was on

135

his haunches and his boots were untied, and four screw-drivers stuck out of various pockets, while a pencil rested behind his ear.

"I knew you'd like him," she said quickly, and she too blushed.

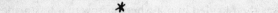

It was a practice of Vera's and Nevin's to separate Adele and Ralphie, so as to speak to them. When they came into the house, Vera would often ask Ralphie to come into her room, which was just off the porch. Seated in a deep chair, with her granny glasses on, and looking (or trying to look) older than she was, she would ask Ralphie to sit down and talk to her. Ralphie would sit down for a moment, on the edge of his seat. Vera had little to say to him, and Ralphie would sit there patiently for fifteen to twenty minutes. Then, walking out into the other room, he would see Nevin sitting down by Adele, speaking to her, about world problems. Adele, her eyes big and wide, would be nodding. Then Nevin would turn about and look at Ralphie and smile. Vera would come out of her room and smile – and then they would all sit together for a while. Everything about Nevin was forced, everything unnatural, and yet Ralphie was too polite to say anything. Nevin simply assumed that Ralphie felt as he did and this was the best way to feel.

At times such as this, Adele looked as if she wouldn't hurt a fly – and as if flies were her best friends – and as if she was filled with the same "non-aggressive" tendencies she had come to believe characterized these new and special people in her life.

136

But when Adele and Ralphie were alone, Adele would be nervous. She would ask Ralphie a hundred times what he was going to do next year, and if she didn't get the answer immediately she would fly into a rage and tell him that he never cared for her. Then she would bite him or something.

She'd walk about like a ghost and refuse to see him when he called for her. But then she would call him up and tell him she had a present for him. She would look at him, and using the same expression as Vera had, she would say: "Why is it, do you think – h'm Ralphie – that only women are interested in the causes of peace?"

"I don't think that's true," Ralphie would say.

"Men have created all the wars – and try to blow things up – HAVEN'T THEY?"

"Well, Ralphie," she said one day, when she was particularly angry, "everyone knows how wrong you are, and everyone just takes advantage of you. I can see it in this here apartment – people always did whatever they wanted to, and you never put your foot down one little bit, did you!" She left the apartment and sat on the steps outside.

"What in hell are you up to?" he said, coming after her.

"Don't worry about me, Ralphie – I am fine. Just because my father is a drunk I am fine. Just never mind me. Just because he forgot me on a river bank and I almost drowned – never mind. Just never mind, Ralphie – "

She sat there stone stiff on the steps, and yet every now and then glanced about to see if he was watching her.

137

Joe's back had taken a turn for the worse again, so a great comedy of sorts took place in the house. Adele had to help him up and down stairs on a number of occasions – that is, both Adele and Rita, with Milly following up the rear. Then they would collect all the pillows in the house and put them around him. He would sit his bum carefully on a cushion, and they would place one at the small of his back, another behind his head, and another on his left foot.

In the middle of the night Rita would awaken to find Joe lying on the living room floor, or pacing up and down. He had the prescription Dr. Savard had given him but still hadn't filled it. And one night Rita came down and sat in the chair in the corner:

"Joe."

"What?"

"If you are in pain – I wouldn't mind if you had a drink."

"I know, Rita, I know."

He was silent for a moment. Under the light from the street his arms were white and she could make out the tattoos on his arms. His body was still strong and thin. His shoulders were large and seemed larger in proportion to the rest of him. He had once carried a piano singlehandedly on his back up Myhrra's stairs and he had also picked up an engine block and moved it across the lawn from its tripod. He also had been a diver and used to help take cars out of the water after accidents. His chest bones seemed to jut out in the light and there was a smell of cigarettes in the room. A pale-yellow half-moon shone on the snow, and branches struck out clearly on the trees a ways away.

"If I take a drink, I'll still wake up to the pain," Joe said and then optimistically he added that he'd heard Tate Reed's back was much better and so he just had to wait this out.

In fact he didn't take a drink, and the next morning his

back was improved enough so he could walk about and smile, and eat a good breakfast.

*

One particular evening, Ralphie brought over a game called Risk – a game where everyone had a certain number of armies and tried to take over the world. Ralphie, with his usual excitement over things, wanted to get everyone to play – they would take sides and form strategies. And he was sure also that he and Adele could take over the world, if they just got lucky.

On the other hand, Joe was certain he could take over the world, that he and Rita had always planned to take over the world, and now it was time to do it.

Myhrra, her cheeks rouged, and her eyes with new eye liner, said that she could take over the world but she didn't want to. The doctor had come to play, with a huge box of assorted candy under his arm, ready for this new challenge.

"What's this game?" he said. "Let's get at it – does it have tanks? I want tanks – destroyers. I want destroyers. . . ."

He handed the candy to Milly, kicked off his toe rubbers, and walked into the kitchen.

The game, with its pieces, and the board, with its eccentric map of the world, lay open upon the kitchen table. Chairs had been brought in from the living room and had been placed around to accommodate everyone. Myhrra stood at the back of the kitchen against the wall, under three pieces of Indian corn, smoking a cigarette, and staring gloomily at them all.

"I'm not sure I want to play this game. I've come down – but I didn't know it was a game like this."

"Like what?" the doctor said immediately.

"Well – you know – a game that depends on aggression." Then she blinked.

Ralphie sitting at the table began to explain the game.

"Now we all get a certain number of armies, and we all go about in rotation placing our armies on the board, taking territories, until all the territories are taken. The best way to go about it is not to spread yourself out but consolidate yourself so you'll be able to withstand attacks, and then from that position you'll be able to attack others."

"And who's going to attack me?" Myhrra said, as she sat down. She looked first at Ralphie and then Adele, and then over to Rita and Joe.

"It's just a game," Joe said.

"I know it's just a game, Joe – I'm not stupid."

As they set up their pieces, both Myhrra and Adele said they were being discriminated against, because it was the doctor and Ralphie who set the pieces down for them, since they were their team members.

"Here, Myhrra, *you* put the pieces down," the doctor said.

"Doesn't matter – let's start over."

"Yes, and I don't want United States – I want Europe," Adele said. "Let's start over."

Joe said nothing. Rita shrugged, and kept flipping an army from one hand to another.

Then Adele and Myhrra started to put the pieces down in rotation with Rita.

"I was going to put a piece here, Myhrra," Adele whispered, standing over the board, wearing a loose top and a big pair of black corduroys that had caught a whole bunch of lint. "Do you mind?"

"Well. . . ." Myhrra said. "Okay, go ahead. I was going to take it – doesn't matter."

"Okay, I promise not to attack you on that side if you

don't attack me on this side," Adele said, putting the piece down.

"Rita, Rita," Myhrra said. "You have all of Africa." She lit a cigarette quickly and stared at the board.

"Well, no one else seemed to want it," Rita said, looking about as if she had done something wrong.

"We should all take parts of countries and no one take a whole country," Myhrra said.

"At the apartment when we play. . . ." Ralphie started to explain.

"Well, you give me a part of Africa and I'll give you a toe hold in South America," Myhrra said. Adele was still standing over the board, blinking her shortsighted eyes (she refused to get her eyes checked, because she was scared she would have to wear glasses).

Finally when they had the pieces all placed, and their armies faced each other, Joe had first roll of the dice. Since he and Rita's armies were closest to Myhrra's, Joe turned to her.

"Pick up your dice there, Myhrra, and we'll go to war," he said.

"Why me?" Myhrra said. "Why not attack Ralphie?"

"Let him attack us – we're ready for him," the doctor said.

"I don't know, then – who do you want me to attack, Rita?" Joe said.

"Come on, Myhrra," Rita said, moving her bum on the chair, as if signalling she was getting ready, and wrapping her feet about the chair legs as if to brace herself for assault.

But Myhrra said if everyone was going to attack her then she may as well not play. The doctor gloomily puffed on his pipe, and everyone listened as the wind rose against the side of the house.

Then Milly crawled up on Rita's knee to watch, and started yelling that she didn't have a chance to play. Then Adele had to go to the bathroom and Ralphie wasn't allowed to roll the dice until she got back.

Finally, when it was ten o'clock, Rita had to drag Milly upstairs, and Joe and Ralphie and the doctor were left alone. Ralphie tossed five armies up above his head, and they fell headlong into the Atlantic.

Sometimes Rita would ask Adele why she spent so much time in her room and why she didn't mention her friends.

"Because I'm much too busy to be bothered with friends," Adele would say.

Adele had not seen her friends in a while. Janet and Ruby had not bothered with her since that day at Zellers. The only one who said hello to her now was Cindi, following Janet and Ruby about with peace signs all over her coat. In the winter Cindi went to the hockey games, and since Adele loved to go to them and screech to her heart's content at the referee, Cindi, in her army jacket and tam, would meet Adele there.

Cindi would always say: "Huh, Adele!" and smile. Her teeth were brown and she had a hole in one of them. She was going out at night with Ruby now, and she had been to Madgill's garage, where they had parties. Adele was perplexed by this and worried, but didn't know what to say about it. Cindi used to smile and say as long as she took her medicine she would never have another seizure, and then she would blink her albino eyelashes and grin. The biggest thing that Cindi had which allowed Ruby to alternately protect her and humiliate her was her disability. Sometimes when they went out, Ruby, with a toss of her head, would say: "Try not ta be an epileptic for one night."

Adele, who knew this, was now concerned with what they might say about her, and of all the reasons she wanted to stay one of their group, the biggest was the fear that they would talk about her if she didn't. Especially she worried that they would talk about her father – just the way she had, and the various businesses he'd set up and the cards he'd had printed to hand out, or the time he'd left her on a rock in the river to paddle his canoe up across the rapids and fish, or the time he was going to put Rita's brothers out of the house. Adele told all of these stories with a great deal of exaggeration, with her feet tapping, smoking cigarettes, believing Ruby and Cindi would be eternally grateful to her for telling them.

What if they told things about her or made fun of her and Ralphie? What if they told her father all the things she told about him? How he used to get drunk and wrestle with the big German shepherd across the road – and the things she had said about her mother as well. Like all teenagers, she believed her parents had tremendous faults. All of these faults were visible to her, yet now that she had told all about them, she looked upon them in a new light, as being inoffensive, and as if she, in the telling of these stories, had taken on responsibility for some of the very mistakes she bragged about her parents committing.

Another person who used to come to the house and see her mother was Belinda. Belinda and her little girl Maggie. Rita would wait for them to come, and always have tea ready for her.

"How are you today, Belinda," she would say. "How's Maggie doing?"

Belinda didn't like people too much, was suspicious of young girls, and frightened of her old boyfriend, Vye, and often ended the conversation by saying that some day she would get the police because of the noise at night. Then pushing Maggie's cap onto her head, and heading down over the hill with old kitchen drapes that Rita had given her for her apartment scraping the snow, or some silverware that Rita gave her in the pockets of her coat, she would disappear around Lutes' house, and Adele would shout:

"Is she gone yet?"

"Yes," Milly, who was lookout on the upstairs steps, would answer.

"Well, blessings come at the strangest times," Adele would say, and coming out the door in her housecoat she would strut into the bathroom before anyone else could see her.

Adele did not like to be seen when Belinda came around. But once she got caught standing in the kitchen.

"Hello," Adele said, abruptly walking past her, her face as stern as ever, and her hair bouncing up and down on her head.

Belinda looked at her and nodded. Belinda always dressed her daughter as best she could. Maggie's ears were pierced, and her chubby neck was adorned by a silver necklace. Every day there would be a new outfit.

Adele didn't like the little girl either. But Adele didn't like any of these kids her mother kept three days a week. "I can't do nothing," she would screech, and then shove one of the culprits on his arse. "I'm trying to study for my project (it was always a project when she wanted to emphasize the importance of her school work) but I'll flunk for

144

sure with all these screamin-meemies all over the place."

Rita would go about picking up kids and toys, with her blouse half undone, and her hair hanging limply in a ponytail. Whenever her mother tried to explain something to her, Adele would yawn, and look about as if she were thinking of something else entirely.

Adele used to like to wear leotards about the house. But now she had suddenly become very modest.

Milly would come from the bathroom with her pants down, yelling: "I gotta find some kleenest – ta wipe my bum," and walk past the kitchen table to the cupboard. Rita would walk about with the zipper broken on her pants and a safety pin through it, so when she moved a certain way and leaned against the counter to light a cigarette in the middle of the afternoon, you could see her yellow panties. But Adele, who used to walk about in her tight leotards had now turned modest. At any word or any saying that was sexual or even slightly off-colour, she would now give a start, grow rigid, and look severe.

This was around the time Adele began going to church every morning. Waking up in the cold room, with her new picture of Pete Mahovlich over her bed, she would dress in the cold. It was a cold that made the dust seem heavy, and the house filled with sleep. She could hear Milly snoring in the little bedroom down the hall. At the very end of the hall there was a flush, which they called the bathroom though the main bathroom was downstairs off the kitchen. She would sit down and have a pee, and yawn and blink, and listen to how loudly Milly snored. Then she would think of the cartoons she'd seen, where the roof lifted when the

145

family snored, and this thought for some reason would displease her.

Then she would go out the front door. The trees would sit heavy in the dark. There was still a doorway light on at Myhrra's trailer. And she would walk in the cold darkness up her street to the highway. Here the wind would hit her – she would count her steps along the sidewalk that was just a single pathway.

The huge church was almost empty. Father Dolan, or Father Garret would say mass, the altar boy would glumly do his duty – candles would flicker in the early morning light. Adele would step up to the altar nervously to receive communion.

"The body of Christ," the priest would say.

"Amen – amen," Adele would whisper, staring wide-eyed at this moment, and looking quickly at the marble crucifix. Then she would turn and walk away, her skirt hanging below her knees, walking on her run-down heels.

19

Ralphie went to sleep on the chesterfield with a grey blanket over him and his boots still on. Snow blew against the window, and he could smell snow and wood in the alley below. The grey blanket was one which had caught on fire so it had a large hole in it. He slept with his shirt and sweater on – that is, he went to bed with them on but at times he would wake up during the middle of the night and strip some of these things off, throwing them into the corner. He was generally unconscious of doing this, and would wake up in the morning and go about searching for things he had thrown away during the night.

In the mornings the wind rattled the far window where he had stuffed a piece of plastic, and he would wake to the neighbours' footsteps on the landing. Sometimes a thought would come to him and he would get up, and still half asleep would feel about the floor until he found a screw or a bolt, and without even putting his shirt on, though the room was freezing, and walking about on his haunches, he would begin to fix an appliance for someone, with new resolve.

Ralphie would never sleep in a bed if he could help it.

The whole idea of sleeping in a bed was distasteful to him even though he never thought of it very much. At the height of his popularity with his apartment, others used his bed frequently. There was always a smell of humans all over his bed. So he put a crank case on it, and left it at that.

One day Thelma came down to visit the apartment. Sobey's was right next door, and she had been grocery shopping. She came in when Ralphie wasn't there. He was out skating, so she sat on a chair and talked to Ivan Basterache. Ivan told her about all of the times "Judge" Pillar had put him in jail. Ivan kept saying that he deserved all of this, and he was sorry "the judge died." When Thelma took out a cigarette, he leaned forward and asked her for one, and cleared his throat. Then he went about looking for a warm beer he'd left overnight somewhere in the apartment.

"I always liked the judge," he said, with that tone of voice one reserves for those everyone else has a grudge against. "Ya, the judge never did me any favours, but he never harmed me too much."

He called Mr. Pillar "the judge" as if everyone did – and the longer Thelma sat there, the more Ivan felt he could take licence in what he said. He knew very well what he was saying, though he pretended to be naive. He berated Ralphie for his messy apartment and kept saying Ralphie would have to shape up in that department. Ivan told her all about his life, and about his little brother who'd been crushed by a steamroller, and his mother who lived next door to all of her children – with Clay Everette Madgill – and how they'd meet her on the sidewalk and she wouldn't speak to them. Though she wouldn't speak to him, and he and his sisters fended for themselves, he adored his mother. The whole idea that a mother could do no wrong – and if she wore her fox fur coat, while he scrounged about for an egg, so much the better – was a matter not to be argued about. Even though she used to bang his head against the cement wall if she caught him skipping church. "She couldn't learn me nothin," he said, and smiled at his own stupidity.

He told Thelma more about the town in an hour than she had ever known, always with himself as one of the major characters – and always how he was "just about killed" or was "almost caught in a big jackpot" or "nearly had my head blown off on that one there." Then he would look at her and try to think of what else he could say to amuse her, and show himself in the best possible light, with "Dangerous" tattooed on his left wrist and "F.U.C.K." tattooed on his knuckles.

Because she was Ralphie's mother, he wanted to tell Thelma about his own mother. Since she was rich, he wanted to tell her about how Gloria was rich too – and would not have a thing to do with her children – which seemed to Ivan to be a great plus for her. With his straight black hair and narrow eyes that wandered as he spoke, he looked Chinese. He also had a continual self-deprecating grin. Because he was Ralphie's friend Ivan wanted to tell her how Ralphie would not be able to do without him, and he wanted to berate Ralphie just enough so she would realize how well her son was understood.

There was the whole idea of taking Ralphie under his wing and showing him the ropes – teaching him how to catch fish and to poach, and to jack deer, and shoot moose. So off they would go into the woods, and Ivan, with a huge double-barrelled shotgun, and two ammunition belts about his chest, would start shooting as soon as they got up on the dirt roads. He would shoot at squirrels and broken bottles and truck tires. He would shoot at anything he could think of: "Either animal or mineral, animate or inanimate."

149

He had a fine intelligence in a five-foot-six body. Knowing Ralphie did not know the woods, or anything about the woods, but wanted to, Ivan would tell him all he could about himself, and the deeds he had done. Then he would blast off a few more rounds straight into the air as he stood there, amongst the trees that were dying and cold, in his little boots and red peaked cap.

One evening just at dusk the September before, Ivan and Ralphie were hunting moose. Ivan didn't have a moose licence but he neglected to tell Ralphie this. They had gone out to a camp on the river the day before; a small cold place that Ivan was ordered out of the spring before. They were both drinking rum, and Ralphie was sitting back smiling at everything Ivan said – and the more he smiled the more Ivan told him about all the plans he had.

Then they went out and called a moose. They walked straight into a bog, up to their knees in mud, and every now and then, seemingly without rhyme or reason, Ivan would grunt. It was hard to walk, they were cold, it had begun to rain, and, in fact, Ralphie was sure they were both lost.

Then they heard a noise behind them. Ralphie moved around and saw from his left, out in the dark of the trees, a huge form coming toward them. He did not know he was looking at the huge back and shoulders of a bull moose. He had never seen one before.

"Ivan," he said, "what's that?"

"What's what?" Ivan said, shivering, with rain dripping off the brim of his hat, and his little eyes puffy in their sockets.

"Over there – look!"

"Holy – oh fuck, Ralphie – that's a moose."

And with that he started to run down through the trees. "Run, Ralphie, run for fuck sake," he yelled.

Then he began shooting over his shoulder. He slid and fell down, and seemed to disappear in the gloom. Ralphie did not move. He could not. He never saw the entire moose. He saw its huge rack, and then a gigantic flinching shoulder. The moose turned, snorted, and moved toward him. Though the bog was filled with trees, they were all cedar with their branches fifteen to twenty feet off the ground.

"Climb a tree!" Ivan roared.

"I can't find any," Ralphie said, looking about.

Then suddenly, as if possessed – and as if all of his life he had been slightly possessed in order to protect himself – Ivan stumbled up the bank, screaming, with the double-barrelled shotgun blasting.

"Hold er now – you'll shoot me!" Ralphie screamed.

But Ivan didn't hear him. The great bull staggered, slumped to one side, got up again, and moved forward. Then, its front legs gone, and a blow of blood coming from its nose, the moose came down with a crash four feet from Ralphie.

"Is it dead?" Ivan called back.

"I don't know," Ralphie said.

"Well, throw something at it," he said. Ralphie looked over at Ivan. Ivan could still remember his face had two streaks of blood on the cheeks.

Because Thelma was educated, he wanted to tell her about how he ruined his life "in that there" by beating up a variety of teachers, and carrying jack-knives. Then he asked her for another cigarette and contemplated all of what he had said. What he was hoping for was what he always received from people – that they would say they knew he was really good at heart, but he might have gotten off on a wrong foot. This wrong foot business was what he'd always received and he hoped to receive it again.

Thelma looked around at the apartment, at the stains on the wall, at the motor in the corner, at the radios on the floor, and the televisions with their insides taken out, and sighed. She wore a pearl necklace and tiny pearl earrings. She always wore red lipstick, which made her mouth look older than it might have otherwise. Then Ivan went about the apartment trying to find her a clean cup to make her a cup of tea. She was willing to have the tea, until she saw what he was going to make it in – that is, he was boiling the water in an old pot that had, when she came in, been sitting on the stereo with some beans in it.

"I don't think I'll have tea," she said. And with that, she smiled, and continued to wait for her son.

But at this point, Ivan, not really knowing he would scare the woman, started to bang and kick things about. Cupboard doors opened and slammed, a box of crackers went flying across the room.

"I don't know where in fuck he keeps his tea – that boy's fuckin crazy, if you ask me." Sipping on his beer, he passed Thelma and went out onto the landing and shouted: "Hey, Belinda! You got a tea bag? I got a woman down here wants a drink a some tea! Hey, you up there!" And then he mumbled: "Put up with that fat sonofabitch from Bellefond for too long as it is . . . . " Then he came back in, and smiled suddenly, when he realized Thelma was watching him.

"I know where to get some tea – I'll go over to Sobey's – "

"Don't worry about it, really," Thelma said.

"You'll get your tea, I promise. If that no good son of yours was half a man he'd have some tea . . . ." Then he smiled angelically, and went clomping down the stairs.

She sat patiently, in the depressing apartment, waiting for her son.

"I got ya tea – I got ya tea," he said, five minutes later, coming back into the apartment. "Just don't let on where-bouts. We'll just have a little secret about where this tea comes from – or else we'll both be in a big jackpot."

"Oh – I see," Thelma said, smiling bravely. But just then Ralphie walked into the apartment, and she gave him a hard cold stare, as if she had figured everything out, and he had been caught red-handed at something.

"Get out there and make your mother some tea," Ivan said suddenly, as if he and Thelma had decided together the one thing Ralphie needed was discipline. And he walked about the apartment in his old sweat-stained t-shirt, angry with Ralphie as well.

= 20 =

Early in the new year Joe had a job to do. He had to go out to Vye's and take apart the furnace pipe and put on a new one. He had promised to do this and had never gotten about to do it, and Vye had asked Rita if he had forgotten. Rita came home and asked him if he had forgotten. She looked at him as he stood with his back to her.

"Yes," he said. "I'm going over tonight."

In fact, he was going over that night. The worst of it was that he had no faith in himself concerning this. If he did not do the job he would be looked upon as ridiculous. If he looked ridiculous perhaps Rita would think it was because he had quit drinking and had gone strange. If he did not do it he would feel less than himself, and yet, once he had done it, he felt something would happen that could make him regret it.

Joe hated these thoughts, and came to the conclusion that no matter if he had felt injured over something, that didn't matter at the moment. What mattered at the moment was that he had told them he would go and fix the furnace.

He took Milly with him and got to the house about eight-thirty. What happened was totally different than Joe had expected. Part of the reason was the fact that the house, off on a side street, did not look inside the way Joe pictured it would. Besides this, it had the faded walls and small knick-knacks and calendars that Joe had always associated with his youth. Vye met him at the door and welcomed him as if he'd long wanted him to come to the house and was just waiting for an opportunity like this. He also followed him downstairs and stood behind him as he worked, talking kindly, with deep empathy.

"Well – why haven't you been to the curling club again?" Vye asked. And his voice sounded genuinely sorry for something.

Joe, at that moment, was standing on an old block of wood and trying to loosen the pipe, and could not answer. Then he said, "I was pretty busy."

"Oh – busy – you and Rita have to get out more."

Joe worked very quickly, and with the dexterity of a man who is ingenious at what he does and needs little to work with. If something went wrong, Joe would usually find a way to fix it, and never be stumped when most others were.

Milly was sitting on the oil barrel holding his emergency light up to the pipe. Whenever Vye spoke, she would look at him out the corner of her eye, and then shift her eyes back to Joe's hands, which were labouring to get the pipe in place. Then she would look back at Vye again, then she looked at Joe's right hand. His thumb had been sewn back on because it had been cut off on a saw.

Vye asked Milly if she would like anything to drink.

"Pepsi," Milly said, without taking her eyes off Joe's hands.

"Don't be rude," Joe said.

"Please," Milly said.

When Vye left, Milly whispered: "He's wearing his slippers in the basement."

"That's up to him," Joe said.

"Rita told us never to do it," Milly sniffed self-righteously.

Milly was waiting for Joe to tell Vye about the deer he had shot while she was in the basket on his back. But Joe didn't. She found it strange that he didn't. She continued to hold the light and looked at his hands, and then at his feet, which were up on their toes on a block of wood, his boot-laces untied.

When Vye came downstairs with her Pepsi, Milly moved the light and shone it at his slippers, and then quickly up at his funny face, and then back on his slippers again.

"Put the light back up here," Joe said, gruffly, and back the light went as quickly as possible on his hands.

"Thank you, Milly," Joe said.

When Joe had finished, Milly jumped off the oil barrel and ran to the stairs before either of them, and disappeared up them. Then she ran back down and grabbed her father by the arm, while Vye was talking to him about the furnace. She kept yanking at him to go, and Joe kept telling her to be quiet because Vye was talking. Vye looked down at her and smiled again with kindness, and every time Joe went to pat her on the head she would step just out of reach.

"Let's go, 'kay?" Milly said. "Let's go, 'kay?"

When she finally got them to the kitchen, Milly was still wrestling with her father, standing back on her heels and pulling on his arms.

Joe then kept trying to ward off Vye who was writing him a cheque. This to him was the main point, the one which he was readying himself for. Vye tried to stuff the cheque into Joe's pocket as if Joe were a child. He did not want to take money, and Vye was just as convinced that he should take it – in fact, that he must take it.

But Joe would not take it. They stood looking at each

other for a moment; Joe leaning against the counter with a stooped expression. "No no – I don't want cher money," he said.

"But I have to pay you," Vye said.

While they were speaking, Milly, tired of yanking on her father, began to walk about, as if she had now forgotten about home completely. After a moment they heard a loud sneeze and she came back with her face covered in powder, holding a compact in her hand. "Look at Mom's compact," she said.

"No, no – that's not yer mother's," Vye said.

He looked at Joe, and Joe looked quickly away, which made Vye put his hand up and cough. "No, no," he said, "that's not Rita's."

"I know it ain't," Joe said softly. "That's an end to it," he said, and then cleared his throat, while Milly looked up at them both with powder on her face, busily scratching her bum.

Then Vye smiled and looked sorrowfully about. All Joe could think of was the compact and the notion that everything had to be refuted. What was worse than the compact being there, was that who it belonged to had to be clarified.

In fact, when Joe left the house and carried Milly down the steps, he was certain it wasn't Rita's. But when he got to his lane and turned down it, he was certain that it was.

Shortly after this, Rita fell with a load of wash and hit her eye on the corner of the washing machine. She did not want to show Joe the eye because she was worried he would take her to the hospital and people might think he had beaten her.

157

She packed a face-cloth with ice and went to sit on the edge of the couch. A woman, when she is worried, will either sit on the edge of a couch with her feet together and her hand on her chin, or lean back against one arm with her feet tucked up under her. A man, when he is worried, will generally move something, tap or pace, or suddenly come to a halt in the centre of the room, as if someone has just thrown water on him.

The next day when parents brought their children, they saw the eye, bloodshot and bruised. Rita was going about as always, laughing and talking, a cigarette going in the ashtray. Adele was sitting at the table eating her breakfast, looking suspiciously at everyone, sneering at the kids, and telling them to line up and not all rush towards the toy-box at the same time. Adele this morning wore her hair in two Indian braids, her little face whiter than a ghost, and her nose looking sharper. She made no comment on Rita's condition. Milly, who was running about trying to get dressed and looking for things she was holding on to, and for things she was already wearing, kept yelling: "Take a look at Rita's shiner!"

A rumour started that Joe had caught Rita at the club with Vye, and slapped Rita in the face, and would no longer allow her to curl.

21

It was January and Vera had trouble feeling good. Her throat was sore and she had a cold. Some mornings she did not even feel like dressing but she got up in the cold room, in the dark, and, standing naked, turned on the small light over her head. The weather was bad and they were cut off from everything. When they looked one way they could see the bay, covered in ice. When she went up to town, with its cenotaph and store windows, she only got more depressed.

They met some Acadian friends and went with them to their winter carnival further down the coast. Vera had dressed up to be suddenly Acadian, wearing an Acadian pin, and traditional Acadian dress. More than ever at this time, she disowned her own culture and wanted to belong with the Acadians who she felt were victims like herself. However, the night of the winter carnival, she and Nevin found themselves alone and ignored. People seemed to want to prove how uninhibited their culture was. And when people tell you that they are not restrained or inhibited, and have authenticity, they are also suggesting that you are restrained and inhibited and lack that which is authentic.

Vera felt sad that night because she had read all of Maillet, and listened to Edith Butler, and Nevin had joined in the causes of French equality and simply assumed he knew all about the issues. With her little pin that supported French culture, the sleigh ride they took, and all of the songs, she simply assumed she too would belong.

As for Nevin, as long as he was with Vera, he felt he was speaking out with the right people against the right things, for the right reasons at the right time.

One night Vera left the house for a walk. She went for a walk along the beach and looked at the lights across the bay. The road was dark, the fields above her were frozen and the trees made wretched sounds. It was as if she would be able to stick her face in a fire and not feel it. She looked all alone, like a scarecrow standing in the middle of no-where. She had forgotten her hat, and she stood there for a long time. Out on the highway, at one of the houses they were having a party. There was music from a guitar which reached all the way to where she was, and she could hear screeching, and now and then a door slam, and then loud laughter.

And as she turned back along the road, she stumbled to one side and fell on her stomach, knocking the wind from her. She lifted herself proudly, and brushed the snow off. Far away she could just see the slanted window of her old farmhouse with its yellow light, but tears blurred her eyes.

The doctor had Joe take him by truck and then by Skidoo to Vera's. Vera and Nevin had been snowed in and she was sick, and Thelma had telephoned the doctor. Dr. Hennessey had delivered them all – that is, Vera, Ralphie, Rita, and Milly and Adele. He had delivered Myhrra and her ex-husband also. Old fashioned and an anachronistic thinker, he had one old-fashioned trait which helped her out – he made house calls.

Vera and Nevin lived about fourteen miles out of town, on the down-river side. The doctor's house was on the opposite side of the road, and from his upstairs he looked over the bay, a mile and a half away. He could see Vera's land from his window. He could see the top of her barn and the field, and the lane that led up to her house.

As they came up to the house, the doctor – dressed in a woollen cap and old blue navy sweater with his bow-tie, a pair of bright pea-soup gumboots – took out a chew of plug, walked about the Skidoo, kicking the runners.

Nevin sat by his big woodstove in the kitchen with his hands in the pockets of his corduroy pants. Vera was almost as tall as Ralphie, very thin, with blue eyes and hazel-coloured hair. She wore a pair of black slacks that dragged below her bum, and an old orange-coloured shirt, stuck with woodchips and showing her naked chest bone.

The whole kitchen was dark and spooky because of the styrofoam sheets Nevin used to insulate the walls. Vera began to cough as she stood there, and then looked at them proudly.

It was as if now that they were in the woods they must experience everything, that is, cold and miserable conditions. Joe stood off to the side, smiling – with his eyes swollen because he had had no glasses on while riding his Skidoo, and wearing an old Skidoo suit that was torn at both legs, his boots covered with snow.

There was snow on the doctor's woollen cap, which hung over the left side of his head, and covered his left ear.

"Hello hello hello," he said impatiently.

As soon as he came into the kitchen he looked out of place, where he would not look out of place in any other rural kitchen in the Maritimes.

Nevin was reading a manual on pumps and plumbing, and stared up at Joe. Joe smiled, and tried to light a wet cigarette.

The doctor spit into the stove and opened the damper.

"How's Clare?" Vera asked.

"Clare . . . Clare . . . Clare," the doctor said, as if he were trying to remember her name. "Oh – good good."

Then he got suspicious for a moment as if someone might tell him something he did not want to hear. It was a cloudy day, and heavy storm-clouds sat above the farm, drifts of snow lay against the kitchen window that looked out over the pond. Some far away woods were seen.

"The main thing," he said, "is how are you?"

"I'm fine," she said. "I just got the flu."

"Well, come in and let me look at you – in here," the doctor said brashly, as if he knew exactly where everything was already. And, saying this, he turned, stepped over a pail, and made his way into the other room by another door.

Vera, without looking at anyone, followed him.

"What?" they could hear the doctor saying. "Don't talk about chores – you don't know what a chore is. Chores – a few years ago now – heh heh – I mean you didn't call them chores a few years ago. . . ." Here he cleared his throat as if he was confused. "Having your period?"

And then their voices became muffled.

Meanwhile the whole house was in turmoil. The plumb-

162

ing was broken, and Ralphie was there trying to fix it. Joe stood in the entranceway, letting snow drip from his boots, and now and then he glanced at Nevin.

"Here," Joe said, unzipping his coat. "I'll go down and see if there's something wrong."

Joe walked about in the cellar, looking at the beams.

"What do you think, Ralphie?" he whispered.

The air was cold and stale and when they breathed, steam came out of their mouths.

"I tried to put a new pipe on the pump here – I had the motor running – but I still can't get it to run."

"Who put this one in?" Joe asked.

"I did," Ralphie said.

"Ah, well – no, look . : . . " And he took the wrench from Ralphie's hand. "What do you think?" Joe said, undoing the back of the pump one screw at a time with his huge fingers. "Schooners win tonight or Tigers?"

"I don't know."

"I was on a team once," Joe said. "Left wing. But that was the time I was all drunk – no one wanted me about. One night, I got a plan. I took a gun and put it in my pants, went skating about. I don't know why I did it. I knew a lad from across the river was out to dump me, one of the Monk brothers. Well, I waited for him. I could see him, like out of the corner of my eye, coming in, like when I was in the corner, and soon as he was near me, I slipped under him and said, 'That's enough a that.' And took out my gun – and shot him."

"You shot him?" Ralphie said, with an irrepressible grin on his face.

"Only with a blank," Joe said. "That was sort of the end of my hockey, though." He smiled quickly, and then coughed gently.

163

When Joe stopped speaking, and the breath stopped coming out of his mouth, it was very silent. Ralphie sat upon his haunches watching him clean the pump.

"Now," Joe said, "case back on here – we need more tools – the best way ta do this is for me to take the Skidoo and go back out to the truck and get some and be back, and do this here."

They left the cellar, and came out of the hatch by the rear pantry door.

"I'm going to get my tools," Joe said. "I'll be back."

"You don't have to," Vera said.

Joe clomped about in the kitchen. After Vera spoke she went past him into a room at the opposite end of the kitchen. This was done self-consciously as if all eyes were on her – and besides this, there were strangers walking about in her kitchen as if they had come here to watch her.

In the living room a mahogany table, with a white table-cloth folded upon it, sat in the winter light, and a basket filled with ironed clothes lay beneath it. All her china cups in the cabinet shone cold in the winter light. In that room there was a scent of fabric and snow.

Joe looked over at Nevin and smiled, coughed, and looked about. Nevin had asked him to come and see about a horse one afternoon in the fall. The wind had been blowing from the trees and everyone in the yard was drunk. They had all gotten drunk, as if the process of horse-trading must be carried on when you were too blind to know what you were doing. Clay Everette Madgill was there, with his horse, and Nevin was walking about it. Vera was standing by the back door, looking out at them from the wooden porch.

It was no horse to buy. It had had a heart attack hauling the year before, but had survived. Joe smiled when Nevin said he wanted Joe's opinion on it, because Joe knew instinctively that no matter what he said, Nevin, walking about the yard with Clay Everette, was already determined to buy it. And he knew also, before it happened, that they would blame him for something – or that they would get angry with him if he tried to talk Nevin out of it. The wind came down on the top of Joe's hat, and blew up under his coat sleeves. There was a smell of ice in the mud, and the dooryard looked dead. The trees that separated this farm from Allain Garret's were clear and hard. The horse, left hind hoof turned, breathed somberly.

"I'll buy it," Nevin said. He smiled. Clay Everette nodded solemnly, and Nevin proudly walked out to the barn.

For a month afterwards the horse plodded out of the barn across the field and out onto the highway, where it walked along the road to its old home. And every two days Vera would go up, and coax it back. The first storm, it was hit by a truck hauling peat moss, and lay in front of the doctor's house, breathing in and out, and trying every little while to stand up.

"Well – are we going home?" Hennessey said to Joe after he wrote Vera a prescription and told her to rest in bed.

"I want to get their pump going," Joe said.

Nevin insisted that he didn't have to do it, that he would do it himself, but Joe insisted that he did. When Joe was in the cellar he'd seen the work done on it already – and realized that someone from down river had been hired. Joe knew that he had charged them a lot of money probably, and had put all his pipes on wrong.

Nevin looked as if nothing was wrong with his house, and in fact everything was the way he wanted it to be. He had just applied for a grant from the government to build a windmill – something which was suddenly considered by everyone to be totally innovative and new.

Since there was nothing wrong with their house – and since everything was airtight and shipshape – he didn't want them to fix the pump. He had spent hundreds of dollars since he had come here and now was almost broke. The money that was supposed to last them two years had dwindled to almost nothing already – and, therefore, everything was fixed.

The doctor sat in the chair beside Ralphie. Vera came out of the other room, closed the door quickly, and walked past them all into the far room, and shut the door again.

But Joe insisted that the pump had to be fixed so they didn't leave the house until late because of it. Joe took all the pipes off, and then, improvising, made one of his own out of some of the new copper pipe that was there, and out of a section of pipe he had in his truck. So it didn't look nice at all – it was a rather cold, fashionless sort of pipe. Except it worked.

Vera, with her nose running, and her head aching, and her stomach hurting, was now able to flush the toilet. As she came out of the bathroom, the winter's twilight made a dull reflection against all her jars of spices, and whole-wheat flour, and packages of granola.

Vera's sickness persisted. Her temperature rose and she vomited.

At first she thought she could doctor herself, and for a week she drank vegetable soup. Then she took a cold bath followed by a hot bath to change her temperature, and this gave her a case of pneumonia. Her temperature rose to 104°, and the doctor was called to the house.

After seeing his patients that morning he got in his car and drove down to the lane, and leaving the car on the road, walked down to her place. The snow was up to his knees, and he seemed to enjoy the fact that he was out walking through the field, where at every step he had to break the crust and shield his eyes from the glare of the sun.

She lay sweating in bed, naked under two huge quilts, while Nevin walked back and forth outside the door. The upstairs room was icy, and Vera had tried to get up that morning and then had fallen back down into bed.

Vera's hair was long and fine. Her face was large and her hands and feet were big. There was a cherry-coloured mole on her breast. Dr. Hennessey took her temperature and then moved back to the door. He looked about the room, and it saddened him to see the care with which she had tried to make the house exactly like it used to be.

The doctor knew a lot of people like Nevin, or so he thought, and he was always angry with them.

"Well, Nevin," he said, "I suppose you're taking good care of her, are you?"

"Well, it's mutual; she takes care of me too," Nevin said, and smiled down at Vera – as if to please everyone there with the proper way of acting.

"Mutual – I don't like mutual. Never did. It's all or nothing – always was. Pretty soon now, people when they start to live together will sign a contract or something – if you do a dish, I'll do a pot . . . . Not that anyone in their right mind would ever stoop so low – but it might happen."

The doctor knew very well that Vera and Nevin had

signed such a contract, but he pretended to be ignorant of it. And already he was grumbling and talking to a needle he was preparing to give.

Little jars and vases, and a picture of a woman in a cornfield, the smell of wainscoting and closets, books on Margaret Sanger and George Sand, and Greer's *The Female Eunuch* lay on her bedtable. The largeness of her face, and the bigness of her feet, and the self-important strides she made whenever she walked, filled the doctor, who wore his red bow-tie, with compassion. The doctor looked like an old farmer dressed up in the 1940s in one of those pictures beside the huge bumper of a Pontiac.

Nevin stood inside the door. His hair was greying and his eyes were pale. His red suspenders looked very new and there was a sort of precision to the way his hair was unkempt – and a calculation to the way he looked concerned – which the doctor often noticed in people who kept vigil with the sick.

The doctor said she would have to go to the hospital and that he would drive her.

Then Vera got Nevin to help her dress, and she packed an overnight bag, one with an Expo 67 logo on it, and then collected some books. And, as Nevin helped her downstairs, the doctor stood in the kitchen looking at the various grains, rice, and herbs in her jars by the sink, and there was something frugal about the kitchen which made him feel sad.

The doctor brought the car up to the house and he drove them thirty-five miles an hour to the hospital. The three of them sat in the front seat, because his back seat was taken up with garbage, which he often threatened to take to the dump, but never seemed to get around to doing it.

The doctor admitted Vera, checked the glands in her neck, which were swollen, found there was fluid in one lung, put her on antibiotics, and had a nurse stay with her.

The trouble was it was the start of the flu epidemic. The days were very cold, a haze rested over the river, the white houses took on an immaculate sheen, and inside those houses along the river, temperatures roared, and people sweated and vomited. There was such a low morale in the hospital at this time that the nurses were afraid to call in sick since demerits would be put on their record. Half the nurses came to work throwing up, and had to be sent home.

The little Chinese nurse who followed the doctor about on his night tirades when he tipped over things and acted abominably, and *disliked* everyone, came into work in this way. Always frightened of her head nurse, she had a sort of dark fascination with her own ability to remain four foot eleven and keep going. She had restarted truckers' hearts after they'd come in with heart attacks, she had helped in the burn unit. She had given injections of morphine to the dying, and she had dodged things Dr. Hennessey had knocked over. She was named Rose Wong, and the doctor once said to her: "Yes of course you Rose Wong – because if you ever Rose Right we might get something done around this goddamn hospital!"

But even she could not keep going now. The outpatient ward was filled. People lay about in various attitudes, all seeming angry at their own impotence. When one man came in, he was escorted to a bed in the holding-unit. Lying down still in his clothes, and looking up at her, he asked what it was he had.

"Asian flu," she said, smiling down at him.

The sound of wind hit the window at gale force, the top of the snow was washing back and forth.

At the lowest point Vera was delirious and had to be bathed every few hours. They had to drain her left lung but

169

unfortunately, after this procedure, her lung collapsed. Then there was worry about persistent infection – and, as Dr. Hennessey kept saying whenever he saw Thelma: "All the rest of it."

Every time Ralphie came in to see his sister he brought something for her. Her face looked, against her white hospital dressing gown, exceptionally long, and her large head, with blemishes on her forehead, and the way her bony hands, which were rough, lay outside the covers, impressed on Ralphie, who had to wear a mask when he went to see her, that everything they talked about before was nonsense, and if he ever spoke to her again he would be quite different. Then he would bend over and kiss her on the forehead.

22

Joe would sometimes see Vye downtown during the day. He tried not to see him but it was inevitable that he would. Like most rumours, the one he'd heard about Rita was swallowed up in new rumours and things were forgotten. After a few weeks no one seemed to care about it at all.

Vye and Myhrra started to come to the house. When they did, Myhrra would always act as if she had settled a dispute between Rita and Joe – and because of this they were now much closer together.

"No no," she would say, wagging her finger at Joe at the least little thing he said to Rita – as if it was understood how they, as two divorced or separated people, had brought Joe and Rita back together.

But as Joe's back persisted in annoying him on and off and as he felt that he could do nothing for his family unless he got steady work, he sometimes felt that he had nothing left to offer anyone. Since there was nothing much to do in the winter if you were not working and not drinking, Joe became, at the age of forty-three, the same type of man he swore to himself he would never become. That is, he relied on his wife for money – spent his days playing the punch-board and buying lotto tickets, hoping that he would win the jackpot.

The problem with his pain put a strain on everything. Though he was still very strong, he couldn't go into the woods at certain times, because if he had an attack he wouldn't be able to get out. And when the pain got too severe, he couldn't travel in the truck. He would stay at home. If he sat at home and saw Rita doing the housework or lifting things by herself, he would fumble about after her, and she would tell him to go and sit down.

The trouble with Joe was that he was jealous of Rita and always had been. He was eight years older than she was, and he wasn't her first choice. Her first choice was the fellow who made her pregnant the summer she met Joe. She had been in love with him, there was no doubt about it, and he had moved away, and Rita suddenly began to hang about with a group that Joe knew. Besides this, there were others at college she had dated, who now were in business in town, and had done something more than swill wine for the last seventeen years.

To Joe, who had grown up in poverty, who had left school, she was too good for him certainly, and he felt that she would think this as well. It made Joe feel foolish. Once he took to volunteering at the church. He would go up and do repair work, check the building, and sit there in the afternoons all alone playing solitaire. Then he would go home to supper and when Rita asked him where he'd been he would say he had to see people about his compensation, or his chances of getting hired on again. She believed this was a lie, and he knew it, and they never tried to hide that fact.

The idea of drinking to ease the discomfort in his back usually came after supper when he went in to watch television and it would stay with him sometimes until he went to bed.

I can't drink, he would tell himself, when just a few years ago he would have been angry if anyone suggested that to him. *What will happen if I drink*, he would reflect. *The pain might go for a bit and it might not – but even if it does – I'll still be back drinking, and it would make everything worse than before.*

Anyway, he would say to himself, brightening up, *if Tate Reed's back is better, mine will be too, and there's worse off than myself – I should be thinking of what I've got. Well, I can't drink and I can't walk, and I can't work. Can't weld, can't sing – things could be a lot worse. . . .*

The one thing he did after the New Year was start an adult education course at the high school. What he was taking was basic math and English. Joe never had problems with math – he was always quite good at it. But it was spelling he could not get. He did not tell Rita he was taking this course.

One night after a few weeks at the high school Joe sat down at the supper table. Only he and Rita were there. Joe had his sleeves rolled up, and his huge elbows placed upon the table. "Rita!" he said, too loudly, and stuttering suddenly. "Ask me how to spell something. Ask me how to spell Wednesday, for instance."

"Why in hell do you want me to ask you that?"

He looked at her, became suddenly scared, and his face got red. "I don't know."

"How do you spell Wednesday?" she said.

"W-e-d-n-e-s-d-a-y."

Rita looked at him, and smiled.

"Ain't that right?"

"Yes – it is."

"I knew it." He smiled, spitting his snuff into a can.

23

One night about six weeks later, when she was better, Vera and Nevin went up to see Clare and the doctor. Vera had made Clare some raisin bread, which she knew she liked. Vera was still coughing and still taking medication, which she kept in the pocket of her coat.

The doctor was busy cleaning smelts at the sink. He was whistling to himself and talking to his budgie bird about letting him go outside if he didn't stop his squawking.

The night was cold and the doctor's house was never warm. Nevin made the mistake of trying immediately to thank the doctor for coming to see Vera and getting her to the hospital.

"And what does she look like now?" the doctor said. "A scarecrow. Look at her, big eyes – and skinny – she doesn't take care of herself – CLARE!" he yelled.

"I have my chores to do," Vera said, looking at him proudly.

He didn't want to be unkind to her, and so he said nothing else. He batted the back of his head with his hand and lit his pipe, then he put his pipe down as if he had forgotten it completely and picked up a cigarette. He

174

shoved the pipe into his back pocket and, with the cigarette in his mouth, he returned to cleaning the smelts.

"You've just lit your pants on fire," Vera said solemnly.

"Oh have I – have I?" He grabbed the pipe and took it out and threw it down on the counter. Then, because the bird was squawking, he went in and shouted at it.

"You could have had what you should have had, if you had only done what you were supposed to."

But both Nevin and Vera had the feeling that he wasn't shouting at the bird but at them.

"And how's your mother?" Doctor Hennessey said.

"I don't know," Vera answered, just as solemn. "I haven't been up to town."

The doctor continued cleaning the smelts – all the time he spoke, his voice got deeper and hoarser, and the cigarette smoke circled above him. The wind blew through a pipe, and gave the whole house a mournful sound.

"Chores," he said. "Well, I don't waste time with chores myself."

His whole house was a mess. Books and pamphlets lay on chairs, coats sat here and there. There was a smell of woollen socks and sweaters.

The doctor was talking abruptly and trying to find things to say. He looked at Nevin with his cap with the earflaps still pulled down while he sat on the chair, and observed him with the politeness he always reserved for those he disliked.

"How are things at the hospital?" Vera asked.

"Nothing gets done up in that place," the doctor said.

Then he roared again, and his sister-in-law came downstairs. This was Clare, whom he'd lived with for five years, who cared for him and who listened to his complaining about "things out there." "Things out there," he'd said to her after he came home from town the week before, "are getting worse and worse – the worst of it is, now we have people who actually *believe* they believe in pacifism."

Clare – who handled the world much better than he did, and had her hair done every week at Myhrra's (even though the doctor always said it smelled *dumb*) – smiled at Vera and Nevin, as if to indicate that she wanted them to forgive her brother-in-law, which both of them acknowledged, and immediately after this, it became understood by them that everyone thought about the doctor exactly the way they themselves did.

"Who wants smelts?" he said.

Obviously a fight of some kind had taken place between them – as it always did – and the doctor was making amends by cooking something.

Clare tried to take over and he told her to go and sit down. She was a small woman of sixty, with dyed blue hair, and she wore a skirt and bobby socks.

Whenever Clare said that young people were wonderful, the doctor would roar and say that young people weren't wonderful at all, and in fact, there was nothing whatsoever worthwhile about them. And if she thought that people who did exactly what everyone else did, whatever the craze at the moment was, were wonderful – and took poetry classes (Clare had taken a poetry class), and formed encounter groups at the high school, and bragged about pottery cups, and tried to *stop a few wars* – then she could think what she wanted.

Things the doctor did not like talking about included: aid for poverty-stricken countries, helping people in general, seeing to it that things changed, changing anything in general, relaxation (talking about ways to relax, such as yoga – yoga classes in general), anything that had to do with believing that you could change the system – systems in general.

But it didn't matter if Vera or Nevin ever mentioned any of these subjects – though, in fact, they never did – the doctor would still complain about something to himself; the tone of their voice or something. And though he tried to be pleasant to them, he often found himself bursting out in irritation.

As Clare and Vera and Nevin were talking, the aroma of smelts filled the room. Vera hadn't eaten them since she was a little girl. In fact, she had started not to eat meat or fish since the first year of Greenpeace and the protest against the seal hunt. But now the smelts cooking in flour and butter made her want them. But she was afraid to ask. If she asked, the doctor might think the worst of her – this is what went through her mind – so she sat in the kitchen enduring the smell and looked at the clock over the sink, and the other clock over the fridge, and the clock on the timer on the stove – all telling a different time.

Then Clare mentioned the new rule in church about having to stand at the altar to receive, and wondered if Vera liked that idea. Vera was aggravated that Clare did not know what was apparent. Vera was sure her atheism was the one thing that would be apparent. With her big muk-luks on and her coat tied with string, she glanced at Nevin for support. Then she said that she did not think of church very often. Nevin shrugged and said: "And I'm Protestant." And then he looked as if he'd just said something humor-ous. To Nevin, Catholicism was the one religion everyone was now allowed to dismiss.

The doctor felt they were making light of Clare, and he did what he always did to protect her: he told her to shut up and stop bothering people – and eat her smelts and go to bed.

Then he asked Vera and Nevin if they wanted smelts and set out two platesful on the table. He then moved some clothes off a chair and sat down himself.

His clothes were strung all over the house. Clare had done his housework for years until he read an article that hinted that men would not be able to exist without women doing "everything domestic for them," and last month he reacted to this by telling her that he didn't want her to do anything for him. Now he left his clothes everywhere. He had lost airline tickets when he was supposed to fly to a medical convention (he didn't want to go anyway), and had criticized her for not being "orderly." And he cooked all his own meals. All of this was driving her crazy.

The doctor stabbed at his smelts, opened them with his fingers, taking the backbone out and leaving it on the table beside him, doused some vinegar on one and popped it in his mouth. In his pockets there was snuff (for the woods), pipes (for the office), and cigarettes (on hand when he was too lazy to clean his pipe).

As the doctor passed the smelts around, Clare talked of the wedding that was announced between Vye and Myhrra, and how happy she was that Myhrra was getting a chance to be happy. The doctor again frowned, again thought Nevin and Vera would make fun of her, and again came to her aid by telling her that she was crazy, and that no one was ever happy in a marriage – and he could cite a thousand marriages and not find a happy one.

What the doctor said, and how he said it, had the desired effect. Both Nevin and Vera realized how insulting he was to his sister-in-law, and so disarmed the very things they themselves thought. Clare then stood and made some tea – of which Vera would have a cup if it was black.

"Frugality and fasting," the doctor said. "That's how to live life – eh, Vera – not like us gluttons," he said taking another smelt.

"Fasting," he said again, and Vera smiled, looked over at

Nevin, as if by not taking the smelt that she wanted, and drinking tea black, which she never did, she showed him all that she was.

*

The doctor was thinking of retiring soon and starting his "other occupation" which was fly-fishing, but each month the hospital, with its grey corridors and too few beds, had a crisis, and this crisis propelled him on for another month, much to the agitation of those about him.

His biggest concern at this time, and something which if you looked at him you would think he was not capable of being concerned over – because one only had to go back to the volunteer program to see what a misogynist he was, and remember how he told his own sister-in-law Clare to go home and stop bothering the patients by being so nice to them – his one concern was that nurses who did their work fairly be treated with fairness.

The doctor had always seen the same things during an accident or crisis in the hospital. Noting everything about him, wearing his bow-tie and his thick black glasses, he could see not only concern on the faces of the bereaved but an excitement caused by impending death in those about him. For this, he disagreed with the volunteer system because it gave voyeurs of death a legitimacy to bother the bereaved. Also, people could be *selective* about what they volunteered for, and he could not see volunteering for one thing because you were altruistic and not another.

Often because of insomnia he would be awake all night and sleep from noon till late afternoon. Drawing on his strength to get up as soon as he woke, he would toss the blanket off him and stand. He often slept in his pants, and his bare chest still showed signs of being powerful. He would listen to the school bus rattling past, and, looking out the window, he would see snow escaping in great blows over the back fence, and the school kids walking home across the snowed-in driveways under the metallic grey-blue sky.

Then he would wash and shave in his own sink in his bedroom, check the window again and see the sun, pink against the black spruce far away, and see the poplar shoots almost covered in snow. Then he would turn on the portable TV in the corner and watch the last fifteen minutes of his soap opera, "The Edge of Night."

Sometimes he would insult his sister-in-law and make her cry, and then he would feel sorry for her, and would try to make amends. But there was this difference in temperament between them. She, at sixty, perhaps because she was widowed and childless, had suddenly seemed to find a lot to do joining the Gilbert and Sullivan group and the Historical Society. The doctor had always thought of these societies as being a pretence to authenticity that people mistook as cultured and devoted no real time to anyhow. And he disliked them. Yet he still queried her a lot about them.

"Was Roy at the meeting tonight?"

"Yes."

"Of course he would be – that's the kind of society he likes – those kind of societies."

"What kind of societies?"

"All those kind – where you eat little sandwiches – those kind – musical societies. He wanted to start a barbershop quartet here, well, it didn't work, and now it's historical societies. Find out what Virginian Loyalist came here in 1785 – which has nothing to do with me or you being Irish and Scots, but is considered our heritage at any rate."

"Well," said Clare, "why don't you join the Irish or Scottish societies? They hold great parties every year."

"I hate them – I hate everything to do with them – and there isn't one bit of authenticity in them. And I certainly don't need someone from Dublin coming here to tell me where I came from and quote some Irish poet so everyone can think they're cultured. I'd rather be shot in the head or strangled in my sleep."

The trouble with this conversation was that it went on not once but a half dozen times a month. Clare had also taken a concern over Nevin and Vera, whom she loved, and the doctor felt for some reason because of this that he had been betrayed. They came to the house more, and everytime they came to the house the same feeling of being betrayed by something would overwhelm him as Clare smiled and fretted about. It was, in fact, because of this that Nevin believed the doctor to be the most prejudiced person he had ever met. Or at least a man on the wrong side of progress.

But what got the doctor into trouble was his feeling of a deeper reasoning under a surface reason in whatever people said. It sometimes made him cynical whenever anyone else was applauding someone's virtue, and at times it made him act kind toward those who had just done something that was considered disgraceful. His fault lay in his high moral tone when trying to protect anyone others condemned. Nevin did not know the doctor had already sternly reprimanded two women from the Ladies Aid Society at the church for gossiping about him and Vera, saying that Vera and Nevin had every right to live exactly the way they chose.

One night he made the mistake of showing Nevin and Vera Clare's poem: "To Love Oh to Love," which was written in memory of her husband. This, even though Clare

181

begged him not to show it. "Show it!" he roared. "I guess I'll show it – she's a regular JOHN KEEEATS, or something." He had no idea why he said this.

The doctor was sitting off the pantry tying a gigantic streamer fly, but because they had mentioned poetry he, by sudden impulse, went upstairs and found her green poetry folder and brought it down. It had been a long time – five years since she'd written a poem. For a year after her husband died she had tried to find something to do, and she wrote poems.

The doctor came downstairs and Clare blushed and closed her eyes. Then he handed the lined page to Vera to read and stood over her looking down, puffing dramatically on his big round-bowled pipe.

Vera read the poem and without commenting passed it back to him.

"Not a bad poem," the doctor said, embarrassed at Vera's silence.

Clare smiled at them as if frightened. Finally the doctor handed the page to Nevin. Nevin read it, looked over the page, and handed it to Clare, who held it in her hand, fumbled with it, and smiled.

"It's an awful poem," Clare said in a false tone.

"Oh no." Vera said. "It isn't."

The doctor, without wanting to, imitated the exact tone of Clare's voice. "Terrible poem," he said. He knew nothing about poetry and felt absolutely foolish over this decision to show Clare's poem. Now he knew this was all his fault and he was angry. "Mrs. Shakespeare." He laughed unnaturally. "Good enough poem – ha ha."

What relieved the anguish was that old Allain Garret came in to share a talk and a half pint of rum with the doctor.

Some time later, the doctor argued with Clare over being

the sort of old woman who would end up being a Buddhist and writing poems. "What do they agree with that I agree with – nothing whatsoever! And what do I agree with that they do – less than that. They have no idea about moose and have never seen one – and yet chastise anyone for hunting them. They make a mockery of Remembrance Day because they know nothing about it, and it's the same way with their peace movement. In this they believe they are visionaries. That is, they see what is obvious and are visionaries while those who have suffered and loved more (here he could not help thinking of Clare) get no credit at all – well, so what. That's the best way to have it good for them!"

That is how the doctor spoke to Clare all that winter. He told her she was thinking like a tourist. This is because she was becoming interested in crafts – and of all things the doctor hated, crafts were foremost. And again he would not say why he disliked them.

Since Clare never knew how to answer these outbursts, she kept silent. Sometimes the doctor would come home from the hospital and sit in the hallway upstairs rocking and smoking his pipe. Clare would hear that he had shouted at Doctor Savard or had insulted someone.

The doctor knew exactly what made him disagree with Savard at certain times. And it had nothing to do with the French and English question. However, it was simply assumed by everyone that it was the French and English question – that he was a bigot.

The doctor found himself at an age when he shouldn't have to explain anything of how he thought or felt, of explaining nothing on principle. Much like Joe when it came to reconciling himself with his past.

One day Vera went out by herself to cut more wood. She took the chainsaw and walked up the road, and into the back lot of Allain Garret's. The day was mild and the snow was deep, and it filled her rubber boots. The snow was blue under the trees, and hard there also. The sun was warm, the sky pulpy, which always gave Vera a strange feeling, as if the woods would come over her.

The smell of sawdust and oil that caked the top of the saw filled her with that sort of dread of all the mind-numbing, aching work that lay in front of her. She had her hair piled up under her old hat, that came to the top of her dark eyes. In this way she worked for two hours straight. And as she worked, anyone could see that in her thin, tall body lay a great strength and domineering will.

Hearing the saw old Allain came down to speak with her. He rolled one cigarette and then another, sitting on a maple tree fall, as at home here, with his shirt open, and a toque on his head, as at any time in his life. His pockets were filled with bread and he would lift them up and moosebirds would land on his head. He'd smile, without any teeth, then he would flip the bread up and the birds would scatter here and there.

Old Allain told Vera how he had gotten in trouble with a truckload of pigs. He had been taking them down river for a friend. The pigs were squashed into the back of the truck and the door was loose, and every time he went around a corner, a pig or two would fall out. The police eventually stopped him and laid a charge, and he was taken to court. The police claimed that too many of them were squashed together. But Allain had not put the pigs in the truck – the man who owned them had. The expert witness for the defence, a friend of Allain's, said that he saw nothing wrong with the way the pigs were handled whatsoever. That was until he got on the stand.

"Would you load pigs like that?" he was asked.

Allain's friend looked at the picture that the police had taken, looked at the people in the courtroom, looked over at Allain, and shook his head as if suddenly frightened.

"No," he said. "I'd never put a pig into a scrape like that."

Allain's lawyer tried to get him to change his mind, and tried also to make him say what he had in private. But the man, now confused and somewhat ashamed, mumbled that he'd never seen so many pigs "in such a state."

The judge, feeling that this was an excellent opportunity to show where he stood on the subject of cruelty to animals, which was popular, gave a lecture to the defence lawyer – and to the court at large – and complimented Allain's friend, who still looked frightened.

Allain's friend, after he had betrayed Allain about these pigs, looked as if he was angry with Allain and had been for a long time and could not now forgive him. Allain was fined five hundred dollars. Allain did not know what to do. Every year he got two thousand chicks from the fellow, but now he didn't know whether to or not. He thought his friend must be angry with him, though he didn't understand why. They were both seventy years old, and what in god's name were they doing going to court.

Vera listened to this story and said nothing. She was sitting on the saw, with her legs spread and her boots far apart. She peeled herself an orange as she listened, becoming more and more engrossed, not so much in what old Allain was saying, as by the hair in his ears, the gentle smell of woodchips and wine. She thought of his son at home who dressed in a blue suit jacket and sat in the porch.

More than anything, Vera wanted to become like this old man. She was, above all, a shy person, and would not sit on a saw and spread her legs out into the snow like she did, peeling an orange and nodding her head, with anyone she did not trust. There was a loud crash in the bay. There was the smell of smoke lingering in the bare trees, with the bud tips wet and lonely.

Allain smiled. "You work as good as your uncle, Dr. Hennessey," he said shyly. "I love that – like Rita Walsh – strong as a ox." And then he gently patted her head with his thick dark hand.

She got flustered and then smiled, like a child who has just been complimented.

24

Vye went to see his Belinda because he had things to settle. He went because he wanted to prove to Belinda how concerned he was about their past – and how everything was forgiven and that he still cared for her. Once, when she was pregnant, he had promised her he would marry her – but this promise had not been kept. In her apartment at the back of the house there were Advent candles from Rita because Belinda had wanted to celebrate last Christmas exactly as her friend had. When anyone came to the door Belinda would listen to them. In this way, she had collected dozens of pamphlets, from the Mormons and Jehovah's Witnesses, that she displayed proudly on her coffee table.

Belinda had forgiven Vye long ago – because she was frightened that it was her fault, and she wanted him to like her. She was frightened of displeasing Vye and Vye recognized this.

When Vye walked in Belinda was sitting in the chair watching her soap opera. She stood and grabbed Maggie, who wore a т-shirt and strawberry-coloured pants. Maggie looked at him and smiled, and Belinda, carrying her against her right hip, went immediately to pour him tea –

which was one thing she had always done for him. Whenever he came home from work she would have the pot of tea on the stove. She limped across the room in her furry slippers, with a bandage on her left heel, and sat down again.

The difference could be seen immediately in how he dressed compared to how they dressed. Maggie, who was almost three, was certainly dressed as well as possible – but there was always something faded in her clothes, along with the chain about her neck, and the small stud earrings Belinda had put in. It had nothing, of course, to do with faded clothes – it was the whole aspect. Belinda had on clothes which made her look even heavier than she was – a maternity top, and baggy pants, and a black belt.

Though she had once been very pretty, Vye was upset with her looks now, and it made him angry. He did not want to belittle her – but he always ended up doing it.

The child made him angry too. Every time he saw the child he would remember it kicking its legs in the crib, like some type of messenger.

When he spoke to her, Belinda now looked at him in a stern way as if she had practised this look for a long time to be ready for him. But as soon as she looked at him, she held Maggie closer, and her lips began to tremble, not for any other reason but that she thought he might ridicule her. Then, with the child on her knees, she scratched her right hip, and looked around the apartment as if she was surprised at the cracked plaster and the pipe that stuck up through the middle of it.

Vye talked to her while looking out at the neon sign. The snow was dirty and brown. He looked down at it and yawned. The street was empty, the neon sign was warm and cast its red light on a patch of slick snow by the door. He told Belinda he was getting married, that, in fact, he himself was as surprised as she was. "Imagine," he said suddenly. She smiled kindly, and then blushed. Since she was always worried that he would laugh at her and say *things* about her child – she could never bring herself to imagine *what* things – she was only happy that he didn't, and in fact she realized that in his way he was trying to treat her with kindness by telling her this.

*

The wedding was going to take place at the United Church. Myhrra had suddenly become United because of the anguish over her talks with Father Garret. She wanted nothing more to do with him or his church, and, besides, Vye was United.

All of a sudden, Vye tried to be Byron's father. This happened almost overnight. Vye now acted as if he knew all about Byron – knew why he did what he did, and why he sauced his mother. Knew that he, Vye, had to be accepted, so he tried to reason with him and played road hockey in his suit pants. All of this took place as if they were following a prescribed ritual, not being sure where they had learned it. Byron wanted nothing to do with this and acted suspicious every time Vye was around.

Vye was going to be his father. Sometimes Vye would take Byron's part over Myhrra's and Myhrra would say "Oh – you two!" And Byron would look at them both as if questioning their reasoning, and trying to figure something out.

Vye and Myhrra's former life became a pale vestige. Now their whole new life used new words, went to new places, drank new concoctions. They gave up curling and took up racketball; met each other at five instead of seven at night –

and yet everything was familiar. For instance, Vye realized that he should love her, but he wasn't sure if he did. And Myhrra wanted to be elated, wanted to feel that everything was new and exciting – but in her heart she did not feel this.

With Byron in the back seat, they travelled about from one new mall to the other. Byron, seeming to study them, would flick his hand in the air now and then against the winter light when Myhrra said anything that disturbed him, and now and then he'd suddenly look startled, as if he was seeing Myhrra in a new way.

Byron did not have many friends and was sometimes chased home from school. Some of the kids would ambush him by the convent and he would begin his trek, turning to run across the hospital parking lot, making it down across the big houses, rushing in the twilight across the highway to Turcotte's, climbing the fence, and making his way knee-deep in snow across the back field to Joe Walsh's. There Rita would come out of the door and fend off the neighbourhood. As soon as he saw Rita, Byron – having good dexterity when he needed it – would boot someone who had unwittingly turned away, and then he would rush into Rita's house, with his ski mask pulled down over his face and only his eyes and mouth visible.

"Water," he would say.

And with his scarf covered in snow knobs, and his eyes returning again to a sort of sly dismissive nature, he would move to a corner and sit there, drinking his second glass of water, his lips visible, something like an exhausted trout in a clear pool.

But whenever he had a project going the kids would watch him and be conciliatory. Byron would take fifteen mice in cages down to Zellers to sell them – and the trailer and the world he lived in, which was so different from their

190

world at that moment, would overwhelm them and down they would go with him, watch as he walked right into the back of the building, saying: "Mice," and watch as Gerard took the cages into the stock room and paid him.

Sometimes Myhrra would be ecstatic because so many children called for him. Byron, dressed in his scout uniform with his new scout cap tilted on his head, would be going out to a movie, and all the kids would follow him down. The toughest kid, Evan, the kid he had paid to pretend he had beaten up, would be his buddy that day, and he would (from his sale of mice) take four or five of them to the movie that day, buy them treats, and sit there with a sort of brooding fascination as he watched the show.

Then after the movie, walking home in the twilight, with the smell of evening in the houses and in the poplar shoots that stuck up in the snow, and all the buildings trembling as the four o'clock train moved through town, his friends one by one would fade into the background, and he would go home and sit in his room and stare at his pregnant guppy that he had named "Isabella of Spain."

"Did you have a good time?" Myhrra would ask. He would stare at her hips in the twilight as she came in to touch his hair. Sometimes when the top of her thigh touched his shoulder as she patted him he would say in a defiant voice:

"You're a stupid mother, you don't know anything," and he would reach up and turn on the tank light so as to better watch Isabella of Spain.

*

Sometimes Byron would go to Ralphie's apartment and sit in the chair over by the pipe, waiting for Ralphie to come

191

back. Byron would talk about guppies and swordtails and he would become very excited. His hair, which Myhrra continually fashioned, would sit just on the collar of his shirt. He had now started lifting weights at the gym after school and was learning judo at the recreation centre. His eyes were becoming more deep-set like his father's. He told Ralphie about a girl at school named Gidget. She was a little French girl from the crossroads, and this was the girl he was going to like.

He was in Grade Six and there was going to be a skating party. His mother would drive him, they would pick Gidget up, and they would go to the skating party. He would buy her a hot dog. He didn't want his mother to stand at the rink watching him – she would have to go and come back.

"I'm going to take extra money too – for lots of stuff – and then at nine o'clock I'll take her home," Byron said pulling at his mitts and then sniffing, and waiting for Ralphie to answer him. "She will be my squeeze," he said. "Just like Adele is yours."

"Is Adele my squeeze?" Ralphie said, smiling.

"Sure, I've read all about it, Adele is your main squeeze – Gidget will be mine – I've read about it a number of times."

Joe would sometimes come to the apartment as well. He would walk up and down the street, as if making sure Adele was not there, and then he would come to the stairs and climb up them, using the railing and stubbing the cane he sometimes took with him when he went out.

"Now that I haven't swallowed any booze in a while," Joe would say to Ralphie, "I can feel it's a test of some sort. All the time I was drinking, my back wasn't this bad. Do you think it's a test?"

"It might be," Ralphie said, who still believed he was an atheist and didn't know much about what Joe was talking about. Like all young people, he also thought there was something distasteful about AA that he couldn't put his finger on. And though he liked Joe and was proud of him, there was a feeling that he had to be loyal to Adele who, last New Year's Eve, told him all about Joe's drinking. Staring at the birthmark on Joe's forehead, and his broad shoulders, which looked immensely strong, and noticing also that at times Joe's eyes seemed to stare at you from a place far beyond where he was sitting, Ralphie could see the ruined house, the kitchen light broken, and all the lost jobs and frustrations. Rita's hands. Adele pooping her pants.

Ralphie had all kinds of worries. He had to listen to Vera and Nevin and his mother Thelma, and try to keep Adele from being angry with him. He would meet her in the park after school, near the fountain. By March, some warm days had come. The ground could be seen in yellow patches, the benches were wet. The stores sometimes had the smell of sun lingering on their bricks. Some nights as he sat upstairs in the apartment and drank beer, it was warm enough to smell the tile floor, and the faint scent of last fall's wax. Gone were the parties and the boys and girls. The window was still broken, there was still a shotgun hole in the wall. A picture from *Penthouse* magazine still adorned the bathroom wall, and an old guitar with three strings still collected dust under the couch. Now they were all alone again.

When Adele spoke to him one night it was just at twilight. The neon light came into the room. Ralphie knew she was mixed up and sad by times but he didn't know why. He told her that everything would be alright – and suddenly he smiled. She looked like a little princess sitting on the floor. He reached out and touched her hair and stroked it gently. He kept stroking it for the longest time.

Without designing to, Ralphie had become, that winter, one of the people others relied on to listen to them, because Ralphie always somehow sided with them.

*

Ralphie had gotten a job at the mines around this time. He worked underground, and he had gained weight. Often, he would come straight from work and arrive at the Walshes' door at five o'clock. That he was now doing the same job Joe had done years before made Adele happy. She was happy when Joe thought she would be angry.

After the first pay cheque Ralphie got, he came to the house with a present for everyone, and a new pair of work boots. He also wanted to give the family some money.

"Look, Rita – I've eaten here for over a year, I've been at the house more than I've been home – I want you to take the money."

All of them knew they could use the money, and yet everyone understood why Rita and Joe didn't want to take it, except for Ralphie.

Ralphie, with blasting caps still in his shirt (it was illegal to take them off the mines property but he had forgotten them) and a big piece of ore in his pocket which he wanted to study under a microscope, and the smell of the soap that was as familiar to Rita and Joe as the smell of life, walked about in absolute contentment.

He was now going to chew tobacco. He was now going to build himself a camp.

And all of this made Joe nostalgic. "Is Glen still up there?"

"Sure is," Ralphie said. "He's my boss." And he said this as if suddenly he had a boss, and bosses were good things

194

to have. He drank a beer and handed one to Rita, tickled Milly, and talked about what he'd heard that day – that there might be a strike. Actually Ralphie tried to talk as if the strike was important and he, like everyone else, needed the strike. But he didn't want to strike because he'd just started to work – and he didn't seem to realize that a lot of men talk about a strike because they want a holiday, and after a week or so, are not only wanting to go back to work but are angry with their union representative who they believe got them into the strike in the first place.

In everything Ralphie did, Joe saw himself many years ago. First in how he was filled with self-delight and yet totally unaware of some of the foolish things he said. He talked about the processes that went on in the mines, as if Joe would not know about them. He talked about some of the things the men said as if Joe would not have heard of these things. He talked about how wild some of the men were, without ever thinking that Joe had once been there, and had perhaps been as wild as anyone.

25

Joe had always said if things were bad, they could be worse. When he was injured and had to lie in hospital for three months, or whenever he went to see the doctors – at these times when he found himself face to face with something he knew would be impossible to alter, he suddenly took hold of the idea: "Well things could be worse."

But the thing he had to face was not only his lack of work, but his self-esteem. Because he had not done anything for so long a length of time, he knew he would have to face up to the fact that no matter what had happened in his life he had to forget it and start a brand new life, whether or not he was ill, or whether or not he had the sympathy of the one person he loved more than all the others – Adele.

Therefore, he took a job as a bouncer at the tavern. He did not mention this to Rita or Adele. He had to work Thursday through Sunday.

By mid-March the evenings were warming. The hallway smelled of aftershave and soap, the plastic curtains hung limply. There was a smell of dust in the corners, and a pile of wash on the floor and Pampers in the garbage. Rita had almost taken over the care of one ten-year-old boy – Evan. He lived down on the bank with his mother and his grandparents. He was in and out of trouble. Generally he went over to Rita's in the morning, and had toast before he went to school. Then he came at noon for a sandwich and a glass of milk. After school he came into the house and stood in the kitchen asking if Milly was about. Rita then told him he may as well stay for supper.

Joe would go out in the evening, saying he was going to a meeting, either across the river or on one of the reserves, and he'd park his truck in behind the Royal Bank and walk to work. The trouble was all the old familiar faces – the same laughter, the smell of smoke and beer – would make him remember some of the drunks he'd been on.

But now it was different. Standing by the upstairs coatrack, or clearing beer glasses from tables, he hobbled about silently. Joe could always tell who would be in a fight before the night was over and who would be noisy – and he never minded this. Nor when an occasion arose did he ever hit anyone; some he would ask to leave, others he would pick up and carry to the door. Then at night he would lock the front door and go out the back way, through the alley, with the smell of spring in the dark windows, and head for home.

Rita would wake up, turn on the light, and watch him as he got into bed.

"Where were you?" she would say. "It's one o'clock – Milly waited up for her ice cream."

"Her what?"

"You promised her ice cream."

"Oh," he would say.

One night when he was working, Gloria and Myhrra came into the bar. Gloria looked at him, then looked away, smiled at someone, and waved to the back table. Myhrra went up to him. She had been drinking. It was her shower – and only she and Gloria were left – all the rest of her friends had dispersed and gone home.

"Joe," Myhrra said, "you know you shouldn't be here."

She looked at him sadly, as if she had long been waiting for this moment so she could tell him this. Then she touched his arm with a cold hand. There was a smell of perfume on her neck and her little blouse was unbuttoned one button. She wore eye shadow with silver sparkles, and her face looked puffy, as if she had been crying. And just as she said this, her eyes did get damp.

"I don't know about you, Joe," she said, blinking, so that one tear ran down her cheek. "You aren't goin ta put Rita through this again – "

Joe smiled and stammered, but he could say nothing. Sometimes a man or woman, perfectly in the right, will look and act guilty, and with no reason to be. If it had been just Myhrra, Joe would not have acted guilty – but it was the presence of Gloria. Gloria glanced up at him, her dark hair and black eyes were all he saw out of the corner of his eye.

"Come on," Gloria said. "Let's go and get a table there with Peter. Don't worry, Joe," she said, "you're allowed – I won't tell your wife." And why "wife" sounded particularly demeaning at this moment Joe didn't know.

*

They found out that Joe was a bouncer because he came home one night with his head cut open from the claws of a hammer. It was during the liquor strike and boys were running truckloads of beer from the border. In the yard, with the smell of cigars faint in the snow, he was tackled – someone thought Joe would have the keys to the stockroom on him. When they couldn't throw him down, and when he stood in position and planted his feet to throw them off, someone hit him with a hammer. He fell and grabbed his head, and heard their feet retreating toward the wharf, and the shadows going up over the path of snow.

Blood ran over his eyes and down his face. Rita screeched, and tried to take him to the hospital.

Joe shook his head, and said that all he needed was a face-cloth.

"Crazy young fuckers," Joe said.

Everyone assumed Adele would faint – because she had often fainted when she saw a speck of blood. The first time she had her period, she fell down stiff as a board, and when anyone cut themselves. But at this moment her face became filled with the compassion that always brings out beauty.

"Joe," she said, tears welling in her eyes. "Oh god – Joe." And, without knowing that she would ever be able to do something like this, she took away the face-cloth to look at the wound.

26

All weddings are the same, and Vye wanted everything done the way everyone else did it, including the stag party – where they showed four skin-flicks – and Vye sat with his friends, as if stag films and all the rest of it were things he was now going to leave behind. The talk, which he had no interest in, was about hockey and ball. The book, which showed a variety of things that would happen on a honeymoon, he took to be funny because it was supposed to be. His hands were thick, and his face, when he drank, became passive, and at times brooding. He rubbed his eyes and looked about, and smiled at his friends.

Then they brought a girl from the tavern, who was supposed to take him into another room. Vye went into the other room with her. She looked at him and smiled. It was cold in the room. But what happened was perhaps just the same as most other times. Vye was too drunk, and only ended up telling her he loved her.

"I love you too," she said. "What are we going to do?" She held one of those multi-coloured party twisters in her hand, that she was intent on pulling apart.

"I don't know," Vye said, "I just don't know anymore."

The next afternoon, which was cloudy and cold, he had to go and visit his mother. He remembered the little girl from the tavern, the tattoo she had – and how after a while everyone got angry with her. How her neck smelled of twigs.

Vye had lately thought of his mother in this way: that she was not really a part of his life anymore, but that he still had an obligation to her. So as he sat in her room, on the chair with its plastic seat, and told her about the marriage, he wasn't surprised that she didn't seem to understand. He wasn't surprised, but he could not help being disappointed. He showed her a picture of Myhrra – Myhrra was leaning against a cottage door down river. There had been a barbecue. For some strange reason Vye had always wanted to show his mother this picture. It was taken at a time when Myhrra was pretending to be the outrageous divorcee – she was going to parties, and she was getting a bad reputation – leaving Byron to be taken care of by Rita – and trying to pay her ex-husband back. And yet this was the picture Vye – wearing his red coat and high-heeled cowboy boots, which left hard bites in the snow – wanted to show her, and he was disappointed she did not think Myhrra as daring as the picture made out.

When Vye went home, there was sun on the porch. The place was a mess. The living room was still dark, and Vye didn't want to open the living room drapes. There were bottles everywhere. Cans of smoked oysters lay on the table. A plate of crackers and cheese looked damp, as if someone had spilled a beer on it. He remembered speaking to the young girl from the tavern and telling her everything about himself, as they sat on the side of the bed, and he'd acted as if he'd finally found someone he could talk to. Now he was worried about what he'd said, and if she would go around town talking about him. He sat down on a kitchen chair feeling depressed and nervous.

*

Myhrra and Vye were married. Myhrra cried at her wedding, because she could not help doing so. She wanted everything to be better than other weddings.

At the reception at the community centre she had to go into the kitchen twice and, standing in her white dress with the veil, look up at the caterer and tell her they weren't serving the food properly. Byron, who sat at the head table, clinked his fork and spoon monotonously. The matches with the names Myhrra and Vye on them caught the thin afternoon light. Myhrra's mother was gloomy – and in this light looked the way Myhrra would twenty years from now. The night before, she had gotten into an argument with Myhrra over something and it had not settled yet. Three little cousins ran about the table screeching, and every once in a while Byron would throw a bun in their direction. Every time Byron was told to stop throwing a bun, he would look about as if it wasn't him who was throwing it, and look at his mother in her white dress as if she was foolish, and this made Myhrra sad.

Though Rita sat at the head table, Joe sat at the other end of the room, against the wall, with two couples from across the river, whom he did not know.

The bar was opened and there was champagne. Myhrra,

who was pale, looked over at Joe when he toasted the bride. Vye kissed her, and everyone clinked their spoons against their glasses, and Myhrra blushed and looked again at Joe.

It was late afternoon. The sky was pale white, and large flakes of snow started to fall. Heart-shaped flowers with Myhrra and Vye's names were pinned on the wall above the head table.

When the dancing started, Myhrra and Vye, who was wearing a grey tuxedo with yellow cummerbund, danced together, and then as they stepped across the floor, they laughed. Then Vye danced with Rita. Rita blushed as Vye said something, and then she laughed. At this point Myhrra walked over to Joe and asked him to dance.

Joe and she began to dance, and Myhrra began to laugh, though Joe felt he had said nothing funny, and Joe felt he wanted to tell her something which would make her happy.

Adele sat the whole time looking about, almost as pale as Myhrra. She kept glancing at the little watch that Ralphie had given her for her birthday, although her birthday was not for two weeks. Ralphie could not get to the wedding because he had to work a twelve-hour shift at the mines.

After he drank four glasses of champagne, Vye went over to Joe. He sat beside him and told him he was sorry if anything was taken to heart. He looked sad. His nose had a curve at the front and his eyes blinked heavily. He told Joe that Rita was like a sister to him, and they were just friends.

"Now – what we have to do – is get you a job," Vye said, suddenly becoming passionate about Joe and his situation. Then Rita came over and sat down beside them. She took a glass of champagne off the table and drank it, smiled – her teeth were crooked, which enhanced her beauty – and her eyes were dark and warm.

Joe, suddenly and without warning, wanted a drink so badly he could almost taste the rum. He said to himself: "If Adele gets off her arse and goes into the can – I'll have a drink."

Adele at that moment did get up, but it was only to tack a balloon back up on the wall.

Then she looked at Joe and for some reason looked frightened – a way she had not looked since she was eight years old with ulcers, that summer when they lived up by the station, and there was a smell of tar and the wind blew over the burdocks, and for a time the smell of burdocks and wind seemed to make him frightened when he drank. Then she suddenly went over to the far end of the room and sat down very carefully, as if she had just come into a restaurant.

Rita danced with Vye, and then with one of the men from across the river, and then twice with Clay Everette Madgill. Then she took another glass of champagne and danced again. The floor was filled with dancers now, and it somehow seemed ridiculous to Joe. He knew he looked ridiculous sitting in a corner by himself – but he could not bring himself to do anything. There were two chairs in front of him, and Simonie Bath, with her big breasts and her olive skin, was sitting with her father, Allain Garret. She was "the adopted one" – as they said. There were people from New Jersey – that patch of wood down river – where Myhrra's relatives had come from. There were old ladies with powdered skin who kept popping their cups up for tea, and young girls of eleven or twelve, wearing training bras, and learning to dance with cousins shorter than themselves.

Joe was looking around, and what he was seeing was not

so much the people, but the light fixtures and sockets, and he was listening to the pipes and the plumbing because he and Cecil and Maufat McDurmot had built this centre five years ago. He thought about the faint smell of wet bark in the grey twilight with its snow. The smell of the woods, and its dark trees wet and old. The smell of new snow falling against the end of last month's storm; on the windows the last flush of twilight and the sound of passing cars.

This business of not drinking was horrible. He remembered the retreat and the kindly priest who had smiled at him – himself an alcoholic. But that, now, to Joe who had appreciated it, seemed nothing more than ludicrous. And the music? Everyone becomes someone else when they listen to music, Joe was thinking – they believe the music is for themselves alone even though it has nothing to do with them. Once outside in the snow and without music they would be completely different. Joe felt this.

And it didn't matter how he wanted everyone to have a good time, once there was pain how could you concentrate.

Vye passed by again, and now, instead of speaking, he looked the other way, with his head down – as if they had spoken too much already.

The day got darker and snow fell, on the doors and windows and hoods of cars, and on the windows of the community centre, with its lights shining in little squares on the warm drifts.

"St. Patrick is here with his storm," they said, and they all toasted it.

Myhrra drank very seldom but she'd had three glasses of champagne, and stood in the corner with a glass in her hand, smoking a cigarette with her veil tucked behind her hair. Then a plough passed on the road above and the building shook.

Standing in her white dress, Myhrra looked as if she had

been married ten years ago – that it was foggy and that it had started to snow – just as now. That is, it looked for a moment as if the dress was alone in the centre of the room, and there was a drowsy scent from the roof, with its rust and tin – that three lights would beam out from the community centre, giving warmth, and that as a child she had once walked away happy amongst the blotted snowdrifts in the dark.

Once when she spoke, she looked towards the kitchen where the caterers were eating now, and then looked back towards the person speaking to her.

"And everything was done just right," said the little woman from New Jersey, who was talking to her. "Yes," said another woman standing beside them, who seemed to be uncomfortable.

"And the dance is lovely."

"Yes yes," Myhrra said, dropping her cigarette into an empty bottle and bending over just slightly. Her dress was so cumbersome that when she moved she had to pick half of it up to walk. Her high heels were white, and her meshed white panty-hose showed little squares of smooth skin.

There was a line-up at the door to the ladies' washroom, but since most of the men went outside to the back of the building, Adele went into the men's washroom. She was wearing a brown dress with a bright-yellow hood. Her face was quite white and her eyes were large.

She washed her face, took a paper towel and wet it, and put it on her neck. She began mumbling, as if she was

206

talking in a foreign language. Then, calming herself, she went out again.

Adele came back inside and sat in the corner and stared at a beer cup. She looked at it for a time and then Milly came over and tried to sit on her knee.

"Go away," Adele said in a weak voice. She stood and started towards the back door, stumbling slightly from side to side, and then holding onto the edge of the bar.

"Another Coke, is it?" the bartender said, smiling at her. She managed to smile and shook her head, and then walked a little further. The door opened and a man passed her. Snow blew in and she was hit in the face by the smell of evening ice, a wind in the trees and the naked, flat bay outside.

"Well," she said, "I'll just sit down for a moment." She went back inside the men's washroom and sat on the floor. Milly came in and was talking to her. Her Ritalin had worn off and now she was as "crazy as hell" in her little pink dress. She got to jumping back and forth over Adele as she spoke to her.

"Go away," Adele said weakly. "Get Ralphie," she whispered.

"I had cake," Milly was saying. "I had pop – I had candy – I had pop – I had cake – I had Chiclets." Here she chewed the gum with her front teeth. "Chiclets," Milly said. She had a little bow in her hair, and she smiled. Then, looking at Adele, she screamed and ran out of the washroom.

Milly ran around the whole hall waving her arms and screeching, looked at Dr. Hennessey, who was sitting in his suit and thin socks, with an expression of bright indifference, and then she disappeared back into the washroom. Then, since no one followed her, she came back out, running about grabbing at people. Rita, dancing with Clay Everette, saw her and tried to catch her.

"Wa – wa – wa," Milly was saying.

Watching this, Myhrra smiled like a stern parent, while Milly, her left hand squashing four chocolates which she had been carrying, bounced up and down.

"Washroom washroom washroom! " she finally screeched. And then she turned and made her way back to the men's washroom, with Rita following her.

A man stood over Adele looking at her with a sort of bewildered compassion, telling her it would be alright. And she tried to stand and smile, and kept looking about, and then said, "What – what," and waved her hands weakly as if she was annoyed people were looking at her.

Rita told the man to leave and ask Joe to get Dr. Hennessey. Then she removed Adele's clothing, and the two belts and girdle she was wearing to hide her pregnancy, and kept telling her to lie still.

Adele looked up and stared at the washroom light bulb. Dr. Hennessey came with Allain Garret's adopted daughter, Simonie, who was a nurse.

Rita, sitting on the floor, held Adele's head, her lips trembling.

"Everyone's mad at me now," Adele managed, "but I love you all." For some reason there was snow and water on the bottom of her shoes.

"I'm mad at ya – ya almost bled to death," Dr. Hennessey said. "Next time you decide to have one – tell us." Then he looked furiously about, as if knowing people might object to what he'd said.

Milly stood outside with Byron. Byron, at this moment, showed a certain impatience with everything. The music had stopped and then started again and seemed to have created shadows in the hall that had not been there before. Byron held a huge bottle of Pepsi in his hand and paced back and forth, now and then putting his bottom lip over his top and shaking his head.

*

When it came time for Myhrra and Vye to leave, she had trouble with her wedding dress and Joe helped her down the steps. The wind was whistling over the top of a large snowbank near the road, which was flat and darkened. Myhrra pressed her face into Joe's shoulder and then looked up at him and smiled. Then she asked him when he was going to go to the hospital.

Joe didn't know what to say. He just shook his great head, as if he didn't understand something. He did not know why he had stayed behind when the ambulance went up the road. He just had. The doctor, Simonie, Rita, they all had gone; everything had darkened, and the road lay flat. He remembered the doctor in his thin socks and shoes, stepping over a patch of ice, and then turning about knee-deep in a drift while the door of the ambulance was opened. Rita looked like Rita whenever she heard of suffering close to her. He could smell Myhrra's warm breath on his frozen face. It smelled of champagne and chocolate.

"Tell me you like him, Joe," Myhrra said, suddenly, as if she was about to cry. Vye stood in the door. He stood out of the wind, in the entranceway.

"Of course," Joe said, stuttering slightly. "As long as you like him."

"I want you to like him, Joe – I want you and Rita to like him."

And at that moment Joe could not think of anything except that he did like Vye. And that suddenly, and overwhelmingly, perhaps because of the warm breath from her rounded mouth on his cheek, he loved them all.

"When we come back from our vacation, you and I and Rita and – we'll all get together and be a family," she said excitedly, as they stumbled into the blowing snow.

"Sure," he said, "of course – sure."

Then they grabbed Vye by the back of the knees and carried him to the car. They pushed the car, this way and that, until they got it onto the road – all of them waving goodbye.

And suddenly, Myhrra, waving out the window, said, "Joe – Joe," as the car fishtailed and moved out of sight. For a moment everything was quiet. There were wet flakes of snow, and far off they could see the tail-lights moving away.

"I think she wants you to go with her," one of the men said, slapping him on the back, and Joe suddenly looked about and nodded in complete seriousness.

Then when Joe sat down on the steps, sweat sticking to his chest and legs, he became quiet. He turned about, as if someone was talking to him, but no one was. He looked at the shovel in his hand and the carnation which had been covered in snow, and his pants which had a spot of Adele's blood. He went to take a drink of water which was sitting on the side of the steps. But first he looked down at the bay. It was now freezing cold in his suit with the big pockets that he had borrowed. He would have to go to the hospital; and he thought of this as he sat there. Again he thought he heard someone talking to him, and again he found that no one was. He took the bottle of water in his right hand, and drank deeply. It was vodka.

"You drinking again, Joe?" Clay Everette said. "That's vodka you got there. I thought you were on the wagon." Clay stood beside him. Both men were about the same size.

Joe suddenly pretended that he had known there was vodka in the bottle.

"Not at a wedding – at a wedding I drink."

"What happened to Adele?" Clay asked. "She get sick?"

Joe looked at him, puzzled for a second. The overhead wires moaned in the black night air, as did the trees in the dark beyond.

For a moment Clay and he talked about the exhibition, and who was entering horses in it, and the trappers' convention last fall, which Joe did not go to.

Gloria came out to the entranceway. She said something to Clay about drinking – the band was still playing. She made an angry comment about something, and then quickly looked at Joe – and as always when she saw him, she ignored him but could not be indifferent. Joe asked Clay for the bottle. Clay, who could always act aloof with others, always tried not to offend Joe. They had almost come to blows twice – and though Clay didn't fear Joe, he respected him.

"Of course," he said, "the bottle's yours." And he smiled and went into the hall.

Joe walked back up to the truck and set off for the hospital.

27

If Vye had taken any other road he would have been safe. Route 8 and Route 11 were still passable. But the road he chose cut between them, and went through the middle of the woods.

Myhrra didn't notice what he was doing, even when he crossed the bridge and crossed out along the gravel road. It was warm in the car, the heater was on high, and she was wondering if she had done everything she was supposed to. She looked over at Vye. He looked funny and pompous in his tuxedo, and his shoulders and body looked heavy. His hands were short, and his fingernails clipped to the ends of his red fingers. Vye was the type of man who had never been out of the province and yet remained pompous in his narrowness. He shrugged and looked about, and drove the car down over a hill.

The snow fell down on the path the headlights made. Far off in the distance they could make out a large white pine looming up. Myhrra remembered having seen that white pine before.

"How long is this road – before we get to the highway?" she asked.

"I don't know," Vye said. Both of them at that second felt that they should turn back, and yet, strangely, on they went around a turn.

"Once I get out on the goddamn highway, I can get my bearings and probably stop in at the house tonight," Vye said, talking about his brother's house.

Just then the car shuddered, and went sideways for a second, and then around another turn.

They started up a hill and the car tires spun, and Vye and Myhrra laughed. He put the car in low, and made the grade. Myhrra bumped her head once going up, and was jostled a little. Then they started down the other side.

Halfway down the hill the car stalled. Vye managed to start it, and then seeing a drift had covered the gut at the bottom, decided to back up. But backing up the hill became too difficult.

"Goddamn," Vye said. Then, taking a drink of champagne, and giving Myhrra a drink also, he tried to make it through the drift and lost control of the car. Halfway into the drift, snow came up over the hood and windshield. Myhrra grabbed him, and the car was pushed sideways by a force that was unexpected. The car slid down a bank about five feet deep and stalled again, with its front tires off the ground. There was a sudden smell of gas. Everything was silent, except the snow.

After approximately twenty minutes trying to start the car the battery wore down.

The lights dimmed and Vye turned them off for good. The night engulfed them and the road was silent and white. The trees creaked outside the windows.

"What are we going to do?" Myhrra said.

They had come five or six miles on the gravel road. The last house was two miles before that. Myhrra thought back to the time when she was told to leave candles in her glove compartment in the winter, and some salami as well. She had not been hungry all day, but now suddenly she was, and asked Vye if he had anything on him to eat. He handed her a small piece of groom's cake that he had in his pocket.

Vye tried to make the best of it. He took the last drink of champagne, and threw the green bottle into the dark outside. It landed with a slight *shhh* sound on a mat of snow, and then clinked into a ditch.

Vye told her he would have to go back and find some help. Just as he said this, wind tossed the car back and forth, and it seemed to last for a long time.

"Keep the door locked," Vye told her. Then he smiled. He was not prepared to walk seven miles in a storm, but he didn't know this. Once outside the car, it did not feel all that cold. He thought that if a man could run a mile in four minutes (this is how he was thinking) he could walk seven miles in less than an hour and a half.

He had a new scarf in the back of the car and wrapped that about the collar of his three-quarter-length coat. The trouble was he had no boots, only his leather shoes.

He looked in at Myhrra. "Some of the road's bare," he said. "I'll be back in a little while." And then he poked his head inside and kissed her as an afterthought.

"Bring me back something to eat," she said. He took off his watch and gave it to her, and told her to count the minutes until he got back.

Turning around he slipped suddenly and went down on one knee. His body looked suddenly heavy, as he staggered up.

He walked for a while and it soon became clear that everything was covered over. Sometimes snow was up past his shins. And at other times he stepped off the road and went up past his knees. He lit his lighter and found his way back to the road. Sometimes white drifts loomed up like

214

animals, which he was always frightened of – he had not liked the woods since that time on a fishing trip when his friends ran ahead of him and he got lost. Now he looked about and the trees were so close to him that he couldn't believe he was on a road at all, which had become nothing more than a track, with some old wooden fence posts being the only markers.

Snow. Snow on his bare head and behind his ears. He tasted snow on his lips. He thought of an old veteran at the cenotaph, who when he saw the first snowflake of the winter falling out of an iron-grey sky said, "There's mathematical perfection." And then turned to Vye, who was a cadet at the time, smiled, and then kicked his heels absurdly and looked glumly ahead.

Vye suddenly thought of Belinda holding the little girl on her hip. Even though men were stronger they could not carry children with the ease and dexterity of women. And at this moment, feeling lonely, that seemed an essential fact, though he did not know why. He got angry with the trees, and with the sound of the wind.

He took a rest and blew his nose. And then he thought of Myhrra back in the car and he pushed on. He cursed at the snow and at the wind, and he swung his fist twice into the night air. But nothing came of it. His shoes were soaking and his left leg was numb. So he stopped and tried to pull his socks up higher, and then whistled.

He moved on into the snow and drifts, using his lighter to light the way, and stumbling forward as he went. His thick legs made a path – an indistinct track, as if children had played there a long time ago.

Because of the champagne she'd drunk, Myhrra had to get out of the car to have a pee. She took her coat from the back seat and put it around herself. The snow was deep as she struggled over to a certain spot which was almost bare and dry, under the huge white pine she had noticed before but had forgotten about. Vye's watch had ticked away forty-seven minutes. The storm had increased, and yet in the bare spot under the tree she could smell pine nettles and summer branches.

As she stood there, her wedding veil came off and blew up in the air. Snow fell down her neck. She slapped at the snow with her hands as if to brush everything away. Then she remembered the last woman whose hair she had cut, and remembered how white her neck was under her dark, black hair. And then she felt tears in her eyes.

She also thought of Byron with his fish and mice – and how sometimes at night when they were alone he would put on plays for her. Wearing a bath towel as a cape, he would act out Caesar. That was always the character he acted out, that is, his own rendition of who he thought Caesar might be. Sometimes he would have Caesar killing everyone in the house. And sometimes he would have Caesar getting it in the guts and falling into her lap.

But now as she started back she thought she heard an animal and froze. Suddenly the idea that she was alone – miles from the nearest house, in the middle of a blizzard – made her afraid. One tree creaked and then another. And she couldn't see the car from where she was. It sounded to her as if the animal was coming after her, and she panicked and ran away from it.

She ran thirty feet into the woods and then tried to find her way back out. Snow covered her coat and the front of her dress. A stick had scratched her face, and had caught in her hair.

She sat on a log, shaking, looking about, as if waiting for someone to tell her to do something. Now she did not know how she got in here or how she would get out. Taking deep breaths, she looked at Vye's watch to see what time it was and had to scratch the snow off it. It had stopped. The trees are insulting to those who are lost. People curse the trees they are lost amongst, simply because of their indifference.

The best thing was to follow her footprints back, and that is what she attempted to do. A few hours ago she was sitting at the head table, while the emcee told one joke after the other about Myhrra – but now nothing seemed funny. All the words had put a bad taste in her mouth, and her heart sank as she remembered some of the things that were said. She moved on, but in the dark in a blizzard she only struggled on further into the woods. The pit of her stomach seemed to turn cold.

Yet by not finding the road – and by taking a turn to the left because of a windfall that tore her dress, stumbling down a hill and grabbing a branch in the dark – by coming to a brook and being frightened that it was a swamp, and moving back up the hill – and stopping just an instant to realize that she had lost both of her shoes – and by waiting a few seconds to taste the blood on her gashed cheek – she had saved her life.

For if she had done anything else, moments sooner or moments later – or taken another direction in any degree, or stopped for any longer on the windfall when she checked the time, or got out of the car any later to have a pee – she would not have stumbled out in front of Allain Garret's truck lights just as he was backing out of his wood lot. Similarly, if Allain had not left the house when he had, he would not have spotted her.

Allain at first did not even know what he saw. But he

moved forward and shone his truck lights again, and saw Myhrra falling down at just that instant. When he approached her she did not realize it was him and picked up a rotted branch in order to defend herself, and he looked at her from behind a tree quizzically, wondering what she was up to. Then he smiled, his breath smelling of rum and his face creased.

And suddenly she tried to smooth her dress and looked at him, and then sat down in the snow. And when she did this, he smiled again and helped lift her. She began to tell him about Vye, but at this moment he could not help holding her in his old arms, which were shaking.

Vye stumbled forward with his lighter lighting the way. But the wind kept blowing it out. Snow had covered his shoulders and hair, and gotten down the back of his neck. He carried his gloves in his left hand, which was a habit he had.

An hour had passed but he hadn't come to the main road. He had taken his cummerbund off and now regretted it, for snow and wind washed onto his stomach through his open coat.

Then he decided to turn and go back to the car. And then, after a time, and after falling twice, he came to two roads, and had no idea which one to take.

Suddenly he remembered how Joe and Clay Everette could travel in the woods, and this made him angry at them. Besides this, he'd heard a car door slam, but didn't know what direction it came from. Then he saw Maggie smiling at him, the day he went to Belinda's. He yawned suddenly.

After a time he was drawn irresistibly toward the woods, every now and then stopping to check the number of buttons he was missing on his coat, and trying to button them up. He remembered how proudly he'd sat on the men's hands as they carried him to the car. All of the shouting and laughing seemed ridiculous and sad. And he became annoyed with himself for not saying something more, or better, or in a different way.

Vye had taken a wrong turn at the top of the first hill. He had moved off the road the car had travelled, and without knowing it was in a maze of logging roads. His lighter no longer worked and he had left his gloves on a stump. It was a stump he kept circling without knowing that he was. The trees he touched with his hands were often trees he had walked near twenty minutes before. Drawn irresistibly into the woods, he called out Myhrra's name until he couldn't bring himself to anymore, sitting on the very gloves he had left behind an hour ago. He took out his handkerchief and remembered how his best man had tucked it into his pocket in the church, along with a note. He had not read the note, and now it fell into the snow without him seeing it.

Vye didn't know that at that moment there were twenty men looking for him.

Ralphie at that same moment was tucked up in a dark hole, with his light out, smoking a cigarette. He was covered in ore and only the rims around his eyes were white. Because of his hard hat and dirt, his hair was flat on his head. The last thing he thought of was that Adele was pregnant. He himself knew nothing about it.

He was a mile under the earth and he was considering a calculus problem. That is, how does a person get to where he is from where he has been? Ralphie had no idea how, except he believed it was all natural once it happened. And that there was nothing unnatural or not supposed to happen. So he was now tucked up in a hole under the surface, with his feet on an old piece of pipe – that may have been left there seven months ago or longer – smoking a cigarette that he had rolled.

And Ralphie thought of it this way – at first he had no desire to go underground at all and had not intended to. He had intended to be in the lab. That was the job he'd applied for.

Now he was here, beneath the earth. So instead of collecting and analyzing soil samples and taking water samples of streams and ponds, he was carrying blasting caps in his pocket, shovelling ore and placing dynamite, playing pranks on other men – and sometimes crawling up into a chute with a ton of ore above his head. And all of this made him feel special, why he did not know, and since he had grown into it, it was something he would do.

And as he sat back smoking a cigarette, and hearing water drip, he knew he could be no place else. An object falls, it has no idea where it will land, but at every moment of its descent it is exactly where it is supposed to be.

Far above him, the storm howled, but here in a crevice of an old ore drift in a lonesome little pocket a thousand feet beneath the ground, he saw the lights of two men at the end of the tunnel, and the glow of cigarettes.

*

Joe drove toward his camp. It was snowy at the crossroads, where he stopped to think. He pulled over on the side of the road, and watched as the snow came down over his windshield, and danced in front of his headlights.

The truck engine and the smell of snow made him sleepy. He had taken the vodka, but he had not had another drink of it. Once just after he had stopped drinking, he'd gone to a party at Myhrra's. Gloria Basterache had given him a mocha-ball filled with rum. Yet as soon as he had taken it, and had swallowed a sliver of chocolate, he spit the rest of it out. Gloria had apologized and said: "It's just a mocha-ball – it's not poison." And she swung away from him and announced to Rita in the same way she always had when dealing with Joe that she had made some sort of mistake. Then Gloria seemed more angry with him than ever. Joe had to leave the party and go downtown. Walking about half the night, he felt as if he had taken a drink, and since he had taken a drink, what was preventing him from taking another one, and if nothing was preventing him, why didn't he have one? All of the reasons why he might be able to get away with having a drink flooded over him. It was the same as at this very instant.

But why had he hurt his back in the first place? Because he had tried to do something when he was drunk. He had taken the tractor out after dark and had tried to cut the fire off by himself. He had almost done it too – at least on the section of road where he had been working, but the tractor rolled on him, and he was pinned under it, as the fire burned all about him. Joe lay there, while the fire burned toward him, trying to move the wheel back and forth to the right and left to get it off of his lower back.

Yet it was better to drink. No one bothered him. He had a good time, and caused no one any worry. It was a strong

221

man's only weakness, and everyone knew that as a fact. Besides all the reasoning, when you came right down to it, it meant nothing. Why should he be concerned? No one else was.

At the crossroads the snow fell; fell gently over the porches and woodsheds of the five houses that sat near it.

Why he had come here he had no idea. He had started out toward the hospital but had turned onto this road. He rolled the window down, sniffed the cool air, and had a drink out of the plastic bottle. The woods were quiet. A sash of snow fell over the trees, and wisped in the opened doorway of a dry shed. It was good to have this place because it looked so much like the Christmas cards, Joe thought. He wiped his face and had another drink.

He prolonged his stay here another ten minutes by taking a sip out of the bottle now and again. Then, just as he was going to turn around, he suddenly had an impulse to drive further up the snowy road which he knew so well. It looked so still and peaceful that he could not help wanting to go up there. And, leaving the window down so he could feel the air on his face, he went further into the woods. He had every intention of going up to see his child and grandchild – and to be with them – and yet at every point on his journey he was doing other things. Once he got out of the truck and slammed the door, and stared at the sky. At another point he walked in off the road by forty yards to see a tree-stand he had built two falls ago. When he came out, two coydogs ran off ahead of him. Then a huge bull moose, with its back covered in snow, stood up and lumbered off in the other direction. Joe felt that everything was here, and everything here was exactly the way it should be.

Then he went about to the back of the truck and looked into some old cardboard boxes, some old tires, and under

222

some planks for his snowshoe harness, which he was sure he had.

Then, after fixing up his snowshoes, he got back into the truck, turned on the radio, and listened to some music.

Driving again, he came to the new logging road that had been made last fall, and he had a sudden inspiration, so he took it. He wanted to know if he would be able to drive right out to the brook by this new cut. The brook he and Milly camped near. He did not know that this was the brook Myhrra had met. The truck engine valves ticked, there was a smell of gas in the night air, and the snow got deeper. He stopped again – checking to see if he had his comealongs. He knew he had them but he just wanted to be safe.

He went over to the path and walked down to the lean-to and lit a cigarette. Here he hunkered down for a minute and looked about. Far behind him he heard the same moose crashing and he smelled the wind. He heard the coydogs too, and then everything was silent.

He went back to the truck, put on his snowshoes, and went down to the brook with the vodka bottle in his hand. Snow came down and landed on his face. Here the brook spread under some dark alders. The tree stumps had been ploughed back, and the snow rested upon the stumps and alders. To his left was a pond, where an old beaver dam sat eerily in the darkness.

His camp at Brookwall was two miles above the pond. And he turned in that direction. Walking along the brook in the night he disturbed a small animal, perhaps a weasel, who went hopping blindly over the snow and down quickly into some shrubs. At a point above the pond he crossed the brook, which put him onto the old logging roads. And it was on one of these roads that he started off toward his camp.

Looking down at his feet, every now and then he saw an indentation, almost buried in new sifts of snow. He looked at them, and wondered who would be in here, and then decided that it was probably just the way the snow had formed in the blizzard. And he left it at that.

Lighting a fire at his camp, he rummaged about for a little while, lit a lantern and looked over the walls, to see how everything was wintering. Then, without knowing he was going to, he looked at the bottle of vodka, and suddenly he poured it out into the snow.

He lay down and drifted off to sleep. A log cracked in the fire, and embers burned away.

He woke an hour later with a start, as if there was something that he had to do immediately. Yes. He had to get to the hospital. He put on his coat, put his snowshoes back on, and started out. The storm had lifted. Some dry snow scuttled along the drifts of deep snow, and the moon was just coming over the trees which the wind still tossed and tormented. The wind was fresher and colder, and his eyes watered.

He felt good, happy for the first time in a long time, and he was thinking of nothing in particular.

He happened at that moment to cut along a side log road that ran diagonally to the road he had come up on and to the brook which he had crossed. Therefore he would meet the brook further up but sooner. And as he moved along, with the moon now above the trees, he saw those same indentations in the snow. He stooped down and looked more closely at them. He saw how they crossed this logging road in a hurry, and zigzagged off into the woods. It was either someone in lifting traps or else someone lost.

It took Joe a while to track and mark the trees, and to realize that whoever it was had been walking in smaller and smaller circles. Once he had figured this out, Joe went back out onto the logging road again, and made an imaginary line to the centre of the circles, and started in. He walked in, down over a hill, and there, at a place about fifty feet from the brook, he saw Vye huddled up against a stump with his hands up over his face.

Vye looked up at Joe at that second and said, "I lost my gloves, Joe." And he smiled, as if losing his gloves would be what Joe would be most concerned about. And then he seemed to drift back to sleep.

Joe took his coat off, and put it around him. He lifted him to his feet and kept shaking him to wake him up.

Then he crossed the brook, with Vye on his back, and made his way up through clear cut and slag and moved toward his truck. His back pained only slightly but he did not feel it so much – not knowing the processes of how this had all happened, only understanding that it was now irrevocable because it had.

DAVID ADAMS RICHARDS was born in Newcastle, New Brunswick, in 1950. His first novel, *The Coming of Winter* (1974), was awarded the Norma Epstein Prize, and also appeared in translation in Russia. His other novels are: *Blood Ties* (1976), *Lives of Short Duration* (1981), and *Road to the Stilt House* (1985). From 1983 to 1987, Richards was Writer-in-Residence at the University of New Brunswick. In 1986, he was named one of Canada's Ten Best Fiction Writers, in the "45 Below" competition. *Nights Below Station Street* won the Governor General's Award for Fiction for 1988.

DAVID ADAMS RICHARDS lives with his wife Peggy in Fredericton, New Brunswick, where he is working on his next novel.